HIGHLAND ABDUCTION

2 THE BAND OF COUSINS

KEIRA MONTCLAIR

CHAPTER ONE

———◆———

1284, the Highlands of Scotland

ANNA MACGRUDER OPENED HER EYES to darkness and a sense of foreboding. Lying flat on her back in a forest, surrounded by soft moss, twigs, and rotting leaves, she could barely catch her breath through the choking fear.

She had no idea where she was or how she had come to be on the ground in a Highland forest alone in the middle of the night.

Pushing her elbows against the dirt, she lifted her head, scanning the area, but she found nothing and no one to help her. The last thing she recalled was falling asleep in her chamber above stairs in MacGruder Castle, but she'd been in her night rail. Glancing down at her clothing, she had on a pale colored gown with a surcoat. Though they both belonged to her, she'd never worn them together. Who could have dressed her? She had no memory of anything after closing her eyes the previous night. Or was it the previous night…? Could she have been missing for more than a few hours?

Anna had no idea. Her head fell back onto the dense carpet of moss underneath a large oak tree. She'd gone to bed early, unusually exhausted, after having a conversation in front of the hearth with her father, Lorne MacGruder. They'd discussed her impending nuptials to the love of her life, David Drummond. It was one of the better discussions they'd had about the wedding. She and her father had always had a good relationship until the day David had asked for her hand. Ever since then, something had changed between them.

Her mother said her sire simply could not bear the idea of losing his daughter. But last night had been different. For the first time, her sire had acted as if he accepted the idea of the marriage, something he'd seemed uncertain about from the beginning. He'd made every excuse possible for his disapproval of the match—telling her she was too young, she could look higher, and she needn't make a decision so soon. True, he'd accepted David's offer after a few days, but he'd never appeared to be overly pleased with the prospect.

It was another puzzle she'd yet to decipher.

Of one thing she was certain. Her sire would come looking for her as soon as he discovered she was missing, and he had loyal guards who would search from coast to coast to find her. There was a full moon to guide a search party, so she she'd be discovered soon, wouldn't she? She had to believe in them, because a heavy fogginess unlike anything she'd experienced before weighed her down.

Though she kneaded her temple in an attempt to bring back the memories of how she'd come to be here, nothing surfaced.

Nothing. How could that be? Weak, exhausted, and hungry, she fought the tears that threatened to drench her cheeks, instead forcing herself to be strong. She needed to do something to help herself. While she hoped and prayed she'd be found by her sire's men, she couldn't merely lie here waiting for them.

If she had to, she'd walk home by moonlight.

Again she attempted to push herself up, and this time she managed to sit. A few drops of blood marred her surcoat, but she did not sense any wound. Not wanting to succumb to terror, she ignored them, instead gripping a nearby branch to lift herself to standing. The hoot of an owl called out to her, and its familiar cry echoed the question repeating itself in her own mind. David had told her every time he heard the hoot of an owl, he interpreted it to be a warning about someone stalking the area. *Hoo? Who? Hoo?*

She glanced around the periphery but saw no one.

Who had left her here alone in the cold night air where any wild animal or wandering man could come upon her? She shivered, wondering where her cloak had gone. She was never outside without a cloak in late spring. Staring down at her clothing, something pushed her to lift up her gown under the surcoat. Well-hidden beneath the surcoat was her chemise and sleeping gown.

The thought that someone had dressed her made her heart pound as though it were to jump out of her chest. What could have happened?

Placing one foot in front of the other, she took tentative steps in one direction, hoping to find a clearing or some familiar landmark, but to no avail. A wave of dizziness overtook her, propelling her toward a majestic oak that helped her keep her balance. She fought the need to heave her insides all over the ground, instead leaning her back against the wide trunk to take full stock of her surroundings.

A couple of bats squeaked above her, their shapes visible against the full moon, but they stayed away. Scottish pines waved their branches delicately in the night wind, wafting their fragrance to her as if they knew she needed something familiar to settle her queasy belly.

How she loved the scent of pine. Closing her eyes, she breathed in the sweet scent and silently chanted, *Papa will come, Papa will come, Papa will come.*

Once the dizziness settled, she trudged along until she came to a small meadow. The first rosy signs of dawn had appeared on the horizon, so she continued to push ahead, praying she headed toward MacGruder land and not away from it. The dryness of her mouth told her she needed to find a stream soon, but that expedition was postponed when the sound of horses' hooves in the distance caught her ear. At first she thought to run in that direction, but what if the horses belonged to her attacker?

The truth of that thought struck her. Her clothes were filthy, her muscles were sore, and there was only one reason someone would have left her alone in the woods. She accepted what she hadn't wished to admit.

She had been the victim of a brutal attack, and whoever had done it might come after her again.

Anna stumbled across the meadow, tripping three times until she made it to a couple of trees to hide behind.

How she prayed her attacker was not returning for her.

———————

DAVID DRUMMOND HEADED BACK TO his land, a smile on his face. He'd gone to Edinburgh to find a wedding gift for his bride-to-be and found the perfect necklace, a pendant of a white rose. Anna loved her flowers, and they'd spent some time picking bouquets together.

He'd met up with his cousins Will and Maggie briefly. The couple had married about a moon ago after bringing justice to a dastardly predator in Edinburgh, Randall Baines, an English earl who'd attempted to sell wee lasses for profit. Even so, there was quite a bit of work yet to be done. They'd taken down one criminal, aye, but there were many more who needed to be stopped. The kings of Scotland and England had commissioned Maggie and her husband to form a group of protectors to put a stop to the infernal trade. David was gratified to be one of them, along with several other cousins. Maggie and Will had been doing their best to uncover new information in Edinburgh, but they hadn't come up with much yet.

Once the two created a plan, they'd contact all the members of their newly formed group, the Band of Cousins. Until then, he planned to marry his sweet Anna and get settled on Drummond land.

Visiting with Maggie and Will had been beneficial. Their talents and ideas had invigorated him, pushing his own imagination into overdrive. He had to believe they would accomplish everything they set out to do, but it wouldn't be an easy task.

His friend Sweeney headed directly toward him. "'Twas a good journey, aye? I've been waiting on you."

David nodded. "Aye. I found the perfect wedding gift for Anna, and I had the chance to meet with Maggie and Will again."

"Och, the Wild Falconer and his lady. He's built quite a reputation for himself, has he not?" Sweeney asked.

"Aye, however, most of what they say is exaggerated. He only trains two falcons, not one hundred beasts like the rumors suggest. I watched him train them for a couple of hours just to see how he does it. The birds are amazing."

"Sounds interesting," Sweeney said. "You may fill me in on the details later, though I've heard some tidings from your sire that may take precedence…" Sweeney's wide-eyed expression put him on alert. This news wasn't good, and something told him it was related to either his parents or his betrothed, Anna MacGruder. They were due to marry in a moon. He'd only begun officially courting her three moons ago, but they'd fallen in love quickly. David had requested her hand in marriage a moon ago, hoping they could marry within a fortnight. Her sire had convinced them to wait for a while, just to be sure.

"What's wrong?" He wouldn't waste any more time asking questions. "Out with it. No hedging, Sweeney."

"Fair enough. A messenger arrived at the castle with news. Anna has gone missing. She was not in her bed this morning. In fact, they were worried enough that they wished to search the Drummond keep."

"And?" he choked out. A sick feeling rose in his throat at the thought of anything happening to his Anna.

"And your mother refused. The brother was insistent, but when he was informed that you were away to Edinburgh, he calmed down." Sweeney glanced over his shoulder as if he expected someone to attack them.

"What is it? Why are you acting so strangely?"

Sweeney lifted his chin. "Because I don't like that brother. He makes my skin crawl."

"He thought I had her hidden in my chambers?" The audacity of it!

"Aye, he suggested as such, but when he learned you were not present, he changed his attitude." Sweeney turned his horse around, and the two rode side by side back toward the keep.

"Which brother was this? Must have been that fool Ossian." How David hated the bastard. They'd had bad blood since the beginning. He didn't mind Anna's other brother, Filib, but he and Ossian had learned to stay away from each other a long time ago.

He recalled one journey he'd taken to MacGruder land after forming an interest in Anna. Ossian had challenged him to swordplay in a hidden spot not far from the stables. Their sires wouldn't notice them there—or so Ossian said. David had heartily agreed because he'd often sparred with his sire and his uncle Logan, a man known as the beast. He'd tested his skills with his cousins, too, both the Ramsays and the Grants. They'd all made him a better swordsman. He was proud and anxious to show off his prowess with a sword.

Of course, once they were in the spot near the stables, Ossian attempted to change the game.

"Allow me to choose the weapon, Drummond?" he'd asked.

David wasn't that foolish. "Nay, I parry with my own

sword." As did everyone else he knew. What was Mac-Gruder's game?

"You cannot beat me unless 'tis your own weapon?" A crowd of Ossian's friends had fallen in around them, and a few of them tittered mockingly. "Or is it that you're afraid to use another weapon?" He chuckled and urged the onlookers to join him.

Sweeney had been there, along with a few other Drummond guards, and he came to David's defense. "The only person who asks a lad to give up his weapon for a strange one is a person who wishes to play an unfair game."

Ossian came out swinging then, hoping to catch David offguard.

Only he didn't. David was ready for him and parried with him to wild hoots from both sides. One of his swings knocked Ossian to his knees, but Anna's brother quickly regained his ground and proceeded to almost knock David's weapon out of his hands.

Once he regained his sword, David went after Ossian with a fierceness that had surprised them both, but not because of anything Ossian had said. He'd been fueled by a glimpse of Anna—her hazel eyes had met his from behind a nearby tree.

David grunted and growled, spinning and swinging to the best of his ability until he sent Ossian's weapon flying to the ground. Ossian immediately tried to cover his defeat by saying he conceded to their guest as any good host should.

No one believed him. It was clear to everyone present that David had won fairly. His friends pounded his back while the opposition returned to the bailey. He sent his friends after Ossian's group to keep an eye on them.

However, that wasn't the only reason he'd sent them away. Once he was alone, he said, "You can come out from behind the tree now." He peeked over his shoulder just as Anna stepped into his view. "Are you always so timid?" he teased.

Anna shook her head. "Nay, I'm not timid, but I'm not allowed out here. This is where lads belong, not lasses. My sire decreed that many years ago. He'd thrash me if he found out I'd broken his rule."

"Then why are you here?" At the time, David hadn't known her admiration went deep enough for her to risk a thrashing to watch him in a duel.

Anna ran into the stables and returned a moment later dragging a heavy sword. She handed it to him and said, "This is the weapon Ossian wished you to use."

Anna stood back while he studied the weapon. He sighed when he found what he'd expected—someone had taken a tool and placed a cut where no one would see it, in a place that would definitely cause the sword to break if it were used in a serious duel.

Ossian had aimed to hurt him.

He lifted his gaze to Anna and said, "My thanks to you."

The corners of her mouth curled up just a touch. He could see how pleased she was with her revelation, but something still bothered her.

She was afraid she'd be caught, and rightfully so, for Ossian bellowed, "What are you doing?" He had apparently turned around for some reason, then sprinted across the field, the fury in his face growing as he drew closer. When his gaze fell on the sword, his face turned a deep purple. "I'll tell Papa and he'll thrash you until you cannot sit for weeks."

Anna turned to run away, but David grabbed her wrist. He said to Ossian, "If you do, I'll thrash you until *you* cannot sit for weeks, and I'll show both of our sires how you tried to hurt me using a deceitful move the likes of which I haven't seen in a long time." David tipped his head toward the sword Ossian had meddled with, pleased to see the man's eyes narrow. He wanted to upset Ossian's composure, make him realize it wouldn't be wise to continue challenging him—or Anna. Fortunately, David was much bigger than Ossian and much more muscular, which gave credence to his threat.

Ossian whispered, "As you wish. Get the hell out of here, Anna."

Anna had run away like the sleekest deer he'd ever seen. Aye, it could only be Ossian who had dared to come to Drummond land and suggest he would steal Anna away.

Sweeney nodded. "'Twas Ossian who was here looking for you. Something is not right with that one." Sweeney said nothing more, waiting for him to absorb the information.

That was how they usually conducted their friendship. Sweeney knew that David preferred to consider his options before he made a plan. His mother had taught him the importance of making sound decisions since he was heir to her lairdship. His grandsire, David Drummond, also his namesake, had taken the unusual step of passing the lairdship on to his only daughter.

His mother had done a fine job with Clan Drummond. David was proud of his prospering, growing clan, even more so because it would be his someday.

But he couldn't do it without Anna by his side. "She is still missing? When was this?"

"Near dawn. They'd just discovered her missing. Her sire has sent out three groups of guards to search for her."

David glanced up at the sun as it approached the highest spot in the sky. Several hours had passed. Fortunately, the weather was fair for a spring day in the Highlands. The skies were gray, but the temperature was warm enough. If she was outside, exposure wouldn't harm her.

But what the hell could have happened? Anna Mac-Gruder was not typically a risk taker. As much as he hated the thought that someone might have taken her, he couldn't imagine she'd wandered off on her own. "I'll head home, greet my parents, and then ride hard for the MacGruders.

You may gather the guards while I update my parents." If he had to, he'd search from coastline to coastline.

Sweeney said, "I doubt she was stolen out of her keep. I pity the lad who would be fool enough to touch your betrothed."

David quirked his brow at Sweeney. He couldn't disagree with his friend. If anyone dared to touch Anna, the guilty party would regret it.

He had to find her.

CHAPTER TWO

FORTUNATELY, THE HORSES THAT HAD come over the crest were familiar to Anna. Once the horses came into a view, she breathed a sigh of relief at the sight of their MacGruder plaids. Her sire and her brothers had finally come for her. She vowed not to cry, instead stepping out into clear view so they could see her.

Her sire was in the lead, and as soon as he set eyes upon her, she heard him shout, "There! She's over there."

Her voice croaked out a small, "Papa," just as she collapsed into a heap, her legs buckling beneath her.

The next time Anna opened her eyes, she was in her chamber, her mother fussing around her. She moved to sit up but found herself sore in multiple places, as though she'd been tossed off a horse.

Her mother spun around as soon as she moved in her bed. "What are you doing, lass? Stay in your bed. I've called for the tub to be brought up. You are a filthy mess."

Stunned by her mother's comments, she looked down at herself. Would that it had been a dream… Her gown was still covered in dark smudges, and her hair, partly freed of its plait, was full of leaves and twigs. She reached up to pull some of the offensive pieces of shrubbery from it.

What had happened? Had someone truly attacked her?

As if she could read her daughter's mind, her mother repeated her thought, "What happened? Where did you go, Anna? Was it a man? Was it David who did this to you?"

Her mother kneaded her hands, something she did often. Jean MacGruder was a beautiful woman, but she was timid, especially around her own husband.

That made little sense to Anna because she adored her sire. He had treated her like a princess when she was young, though she had long since come to the conclusion her parents did not have a strong marriage. She rarely noticed any sincere affection between them, unlike David's parents, who appeared to be more in love every day. Her sire only spoke to her mother about the running of the keep or Anna and her brothers. She couldn't recall the last time she'd seen them hug or kiss, though she knew her mother was shy by nature. Her mother was also very religious, and her sire often scoffed at her devotion, something Anna privately thought was horrible.

She vowed that her marriage to David Drummond would be different. He would never scoff at something of such importance to her. They knew how to communicate in a way that brought them closer rather than pushed them apart.

Being neighbors, she'd occasionally seen David over the years, but they'd never spoken much until he and his parents joined them for the midday meal one day. The Drummonds had visited because they'd had recent trouble with cattle thieves. Her mother had decided it was time for her to start traveling along with them. Her brothers had stayed outside, but David and his brother Daniel had joined them at the dais. Sitting across from him had been intimidating since she didn't often speak to older lads. He'd asked her what she thought of whatever they were eating and she'd been so stunned, she hadn't known how to answer at first. Her sire never asked her mother such questions.

She recalled the conversation well.

"Are you so shy you won't answer?" He'd waggled his brow at her, something she hadn't known how to interpret.

"I...I...I'm not so shy." She'd squared her shoulders and

lifted her chin. "I'm not afraid of men either."

"Why would you be? You have two brothers."

His answer puzzled her, but no more so than why she'd offered the information in the first place. She had no idea why it had popped into her mind.

He glanced off to the side to be certain he wouldn't be overheard before he whispered, "Then mayhap you'd allow me to kiss you someday." His mouth curled up at the sides.

The dolt had stymied her, having never been approached in such a way before, but she wouldn't allow him to get the best of her. "Now why would I do that?" she asked, glaring at him.

He leaned toward her and whispered, "Because you might enjoy it. You still haven't answered my question. How is your stew?"

She stared at the brown trencher of food in front of her. "My stew is boring, much like you, my lord."

He broke into gales of laughter. That marked the end of their conversation that first day, but David and his sire had begun visiting a bit more often after that. Each time they came to the keep, he would manage to whisper something in her ear about kissing. Then he'd chuckle and she'd respond with a deep blush, repeating the same pattern again and again.

One day she decided she'd had enough of his teasing and shoved him into an alcove while their parents chatted. Her maid had told her all about men using their tongues when they kissed, so she'd decided to try it for herself. Perhaps he'd stop teasing her if she kissed him first. She promptly settled her lips on his and teased him with her tongue. He stood back with a stunned expression on his face.

"Not so shy now, am I, my lord?"

He made the strangest sound in his throat and set his hand on the back of her neck, tugging her close so he could kiss her again. Kiss wasn't a fair term. He nearly devoured her, slanting his mouth over hers, invading her senses with his taste and the feel of his chest against her breasts, something she'd seared into her brain so she could recall the feel of David Drummond at will. When he ended the kiss, they were both panting as if they'd run around the curtain wall five times. Not knowing what else to do, she'd spun on her heel and left him, but this time, there was no echo of laughter following her down the passageway. All she heard was his heavy breathing.

Two moons later, he'd offered for her.

How she adored David. She spent all her time wishing the next moon away so they could marry sooner, only now...

"Anna?" her mother whispered, shaking her out of her thoughts. "Was it David?"

Anna replied with a vehement shake of her head, which caused a pounding directly behind her eyes. "Nay, Mama. David would never hurt me."

"Then who did this to you? How did you end up in the middle of a forest alone? Who was the beast..."

Both of her hands moved up to her temple, which was now pounding from all the questions. The memories still refused to come back. "Mama, I don't know. I cannot recall anything at all. How long was I gone?"

"One night. We have no idea when you left your chamber. Were you hit over the head?"

"I don't remember being hit. How could I lose my memory of everything? Is that possible, Mama? I don't understand what happened."

When her mother sat on the bed beside her and wrapped her in an embrace, Anna could no longer hold her tears back. "How could something like this happen to me? I was in my own chamber," she sobbed, the tears now gushing from her eyes. "Did no one see an intruder at the gates, in the courtyard?"

They sat huddled for a while, her mother patting her

shoulder as she cried. "I don't understand any of it either," her mother said. "I am baffled. I don't know who could have come into our keep and stolen you away without being seen. It seems impossible to me." She fell silent for a moment, worrying her lip with her teeth, then added, "If you do not remember, then perhaps it *was* David."

"Nay!" She tried not to shout at her mother, but the very idea that David would hurt her was abhorrent. "David would never, ever, do such a thing. He loves me. He is not capable of hurting me."

"Hush, lass. Calm down. Rest for a moment until the tub is here." She patted her hands in a small demonstration of affection for her only daughter, also her youngest child. "My dear, do not get yourself upset. You need your rest. You must have been awake most of the night."

A knock sounded at the door, so her mother left her side to answer it. Two guards carried the metal tub into the chamber while several maids followed them in with buckets of steaming water. "There," her mother instructed. "By the hearth."

She leaned her head back onto the soft pillow and closed her eyes, trying as hard as she could to remember anything about the previous night. Nothing. David's face popped into her mind unbidden—his dark hair, his warm green eyes, and his wide smile. Just thinking about him calmed her. He'd told her he was off to Edinburgh, or she'd send a messenger to him at once. How she wished he were here…

She would never forget the day they'd fallen for each other. Anna had always loved flowers, the brighter and more complicated the bloom the better, and one day David had happened upon her and her maid while they'd been collecting bouquets in a meadow. She'd spotted a gorgeous pink bloom atop a ravine, and she and her maid were discussing whether it would be too dangerous to fetch it. He'd immediately volunteered, and even though his face went pale as he climbed to the top of the great height, he'd emerged victorious. They'd laughed and laughed together after he revealed the truth to her—he had a slight fear of heights. To this day, he always helped her gather her bouquets.

David would know what to do, and she would feel safe and protected and loved in his arms. His touch often started a fire in her that she didn't know how to handle, but soon they would be husband and wife, and they would finally be able to share everything…including the act of love. How she looked forward to that.

He took his heirship very seriously, and he vowed to act only as a future laird should. Though they'd shared many passionate kisses, he would do naught to disrespect her and their relationship. She sighed, as she often did when she thought of her handsome betrothed. She'd never seen another man as good-looking as David Drummond. All the lasses in the land pined for him.

But David was hers, all hers.

The maids and guards finished their work and took their leave. Her mother moved to her side and helped her to stand so she could get out of her surcoat. They struggled to pull the outer garment over her messy hair, but finally managed without yanking out too many of her long hairs.

Her mother's ramblings matched her thoughts.

"Who would have dressed you in such clothing? These two do not match. I know better than to ask you if you chose these things, Anna. You would never don such an awful combination." Her mother's gaze narrowed as she fingered the surcoat, carefully checking the condition of the garment before she tossed it over a nearby chair. As soon as she set the ruined surcoat aside, the door burst open.

Anna's father, Lorne, stood there with a look on his face she didn't at all like. His flared nostrils spoke of anger, as did the way his elbows jutted out to his sides when he joined his hands together in front of his chest, cracking his knuckles.

The man's wrath was evident. She fell back onto the bed in her undergown and chemise.

"What is it, my laird?" her mother asked, using his title as she often did in front of the servants. Anna had started to believe it was a gesture intended to placate and calm him.

He never took his eyes off Anna. "Ossian said he noticed blood, but I did not see any."

"Where? I didn't notice any blood," her mother said, her gaze going to their daughter on the bed, perusing her from head to toe.

Anna looked at her sire, unsure of how to answer him. This was not the man she knew. Her sire was calm and loving, not harsh and judgmental. What had transpired over the course of one day to change so much—her memory, her safe life, and her loving father?

As if he could read her thoughts, her father patted her hand, his concern palpable, and addressed her in a calmer tone. "Have you remembered aught, lass?"

This was the sire she adored, so she answered him with a whisper, because she knew the truth would not please him. "Nay, I'm sorry, Papa, but I don't recall aught before I awoke in the forest."

He moved around the bed, looming over her and staring at her clothing, his hand pushing the folds of her undergown around, something that puzzled her. What was he searching for?

"Stand up, please." His tone had changed again, and she did not like it.

She did as she was bidden, though her legs trembled. He grabbed the back of her gown and lifted it, turning her from side to side.

He pointed to her chemise in back. "There. That is blood."

Her mother gasped, her hand rising to her mouth, almost

covering her one word. "Nay."

Her father tossed her undergown back down and said, "You lost your maidenhead. Who?"

She froze, unable to believe what he'd suggested. Could it be true? And the way he'd asked it…it sounded like he believed she was lying about her lack of memory. That she'd had something to do with the attack. Or was he merely angry at her attacker? She had no idea, having never seen him like this before.

He put a hand on each of her shoulders and shook her. With a furious look in his eyes, he repeated, "Who did this?"

———◆———

BY THE TIME HE REACHED Drummond land, David's usual calm demeanor had completely fallen away. Frantic at the thought of what might have happened to his love, he left his horse at the stables and raced toward the keep, ignoring everyone who attempted to talk with him. Sweeney, who knew what he needed, stayed behind to take care of his mount.

Barging into the hall, David spotted his sire sitting on the dais with a goblet of mead in his hand. "What happened?" he shouted. "Where is she?"

His mother descended the dais and strode toward him, her hands in front of her in a gesture meant to placate. "Now, David, calm down."

The words only inflamed his nerves. "Calm down? My betrothed is missing, and I'm supposed to calm down? What the hell, Mama?"

"David, do not speak to your mother in that tone," his sire warned over her shoulder. He, too, had descended the dais.

He took a deep breath, realizing his father was right. "Forgive me, Mama. Please tell me what you know. I feel like a broken man." He placed his hands on his hips as he awaited their response. A strange thought crossed his mind as he looked at them.

He'd finally surpassed his father in height.

"Ossian MacGruder was here earlier," his father said, "as I'm sure Sweeney told you. Apparently, Anna disappeared last night. They don't know the exact time because no one realized it until just before dawn when the maid noticed her door was ajar. They've sent several patrols out in search of her."

"And they thought I stole her out of her own castle?" Rage and terror warred inside of him.

"I don't think so, David," his mother said softly. "Ossian's never been the friendliest lad, but he seemed fraught with worry. He asked about you. We told him you were off to Edinburgh and may not return for a few days. Clearly he could not cast any suspicions your way. You were not here. His sire is beside himself, and no wonder. We all know how he dotes on Anna. They have no idea where she is. There are no missing horses, and no one was seen entering or leaving the gates."

He rubbed his hand across his forehead in frustration, brushing the long hairs out of his face. "I'm going over there to see if they've found her. If not, I'll prepare my own search."

His father, Micheil, said, "I'll go with you. 'Tis the right thing to do." He leaned over to kiss Diana's cheek. "We'll return before nightfall, my sweet."

David grabbed a goblet and threw down several swigs, then grabbed a chunk of cheese sitting out on a nearby platter. He had not eaten in several hours and needed sustenance to see him through the challenges that lay ahead. "I'll meet you near the stables, Papa. Sweeney stayed behind to round up some guards."

"However many you need, son," Diana said with a nod. "And Godspeed to you. I've been so worried about poor Anna. You know I adore her, but she's not tough like so many of your cousins. That Maggie…"

David couldn't argue with his mother's reasoning. There weren't many like his cousins. Maggie's childhood had been difficult before his aunt and uncle adopted her, but she'd come through it as one of the strongest women in his acquaintance. In fact, she had better skills with a dagger than most men. And yet…his mother wasn't altogether right either. When he'd suggested that he and Anna practice throwing daggers one afternoon, he'd doubted it would amount to anything. His love certainly didn't seem capable of violence. But she'd grabbed the weapon from him and hurled it with vehemence. Anna MacGruder continually surprised him, but that counted as the day she'd surprised him most. She had a gentle nature, but beneath it she was as tough as the stones that hid beneath the flowers she loved to collect.

With proper training, she'd be a definite marksman with the dagger.

"If I need to, I'll contact my cousins to assist us." He twirled around and headed out the door, running into Sweeney in the courtyard. "We're headed to MacGruder land." He tossed a hunk of the cheese to his friend.

He yelled to the stable lad to find him another horse since his favorite was in need of a rest. All he could do was pace while he waited.

What the hell could have happened?

It felt as if the future he'd dreamed of was slipping out of his grasp. Up until now, David had lived a bit of a charmed life as the heir to the Drummond land. His parents were wonderful, and other than the one major event that had happened many years ago—something he tried, and failed, to forget—he and his younger brother Daniel had lived a happy life. Loving Anna had improved it in so many ways.

Up until three moons ago, he'd still thought of her as a wee lassie with red pigtails, but everything had changed between them after her parents unexpectedly invited them over for a midday meal. Anna's wit had delighted him.

Whenever they were together, they laughed over everything and anything. It was one of the things he adored most about her. And her connection with nature was so powerful he encouraged it just so he could witness her joy—riding carefree across a meadow, stopping to locate the most beautiful flower, or climbing through the forest to find the source of the most unusual birdcalls. She loved to ride horses as much as he did, so they'd gone out riding together frequently in their courtship, stopping now and again to collect flowers. She looked like a goddess out there among the high grasses, the pop of bright colors in her hand, her dark red hair and hazel eyes glowing. While they'd often had a guard or Filib along to chaperone them, nothing had mattered except that they were together.

The stable lad brought a saddled horse to him, bringing him back to the present moment. His father, no doubt sensing his distraction, began barking orders to the Drummond guards, while he did his best to focus on the present. It was on his shoulders to determine the best way to search for Anna once they reached MacGruder land.

They mounted and headed out the gates, his sire and Sweeney riding on either side of him.

About an hour later, close to MacGruder land, David's sire pulled his horse up next to him. "David, we shall just ask for news of Anna and offer our support. Please do not do aught to set Lorne MacGruder off. If he hasn't found her yet, he'll be frantic. He may not be here, but her mother is sure to be upset, too."

"Mayhap they'll not allow us in at all," Sweeney said from the other side of David.

"Aye," David said. "If she's still missing, MacGruder should have the place locked down tight. No one in, only guards out."

His sire added, "'Tis a possibility, especially if they have no idea how she was taken from her own chambers. Many of their guards are likely out searching for her, which is another reason for them to be careful."

As they approached the gates, David turned to Sweeney. "You were right. The gates are closed, something unusual for midday."

"I cannot see that far. Tell me more about what you see," his sire whispered. His eyesight had started failing of late, something he wasn't eager to share with the guards.

"There isn't much to tell, Papa. There are several guards at the gates, many more on the wall, but the cottages around them are quiet. The people are working the fields, but there is no chatter." The closer they moved, the worse he felt, a gnawing feeling in his gut digging in ever deeper. Clan MacGruder was smaller than Clan Drummond or Clan Ramsay, but they had plenty of clanmates to tend the fields or work in the lists. This day, many were absent. Why?

He could only hope they'd gone out to search for Anna and found her.

"They are staring at you, Drummond," Sweeney said, the first comment he'd made during their desperate ride. "All of them."

This was the first time he'd studied MacGruder land in quite some time. He had to admit that his mind usually focused on Anna and only Anna. Otherwise, he would have noticed the sparse number of huts packed in together. Because they were so close, he'd been deceived into thinking there were more, but he'd been blinded by his betrothed. The Drummond and Ramsay clans were forever growing, but were the MacGruders? He couldn't be sure, but he vowed to pay more attention to what took place on MacGruder land.

As they moved down the path between the huts, David realized Sweeney was correct. Anna's people gave him a strange look. Why? They couldn't possibly suspect him, could they? Hadn't his mother said his visit to Edinburgh had allayed any suspicion? He lifted his hand in greeting to some, but they ignored him.

His father murmured, "Do not take it to heart. When one of the laird's family is hurt or missing, they take it verra seriously. Any clanmate could interpret it as a blight against their kin."

David trusted his sire's opinion, so he nodded and continued on his way, not wishing to anger anyone. When they arrived at the gates, David spoke to one of the guards he knew, only to be immediately shut down. "Go home, Drummond."

He waved to the man in charge of the portcullis. "Raise it. We wish to enter."

The guard said, "Not today."

David wasn't going away. "I know Anna is missing. I wish to talk to someone who can tell me what happened before we head out in search of her ourselves. She's my betrothed and I will find her, but 'twould be helpful to know where the MacGruder patrols have gone."

The guard finally looked him in the eye. "She's been found, and you're not to see her. No one is allowed inside. Orders from our laird."

The lump in his throat kept him from speaking. He was pleased when his sire took over for him. "She's alive?" his father asked.

"Aye, she's alive, but 'tis all we know. She was not in good shape when she was found in the forest. MacGruder says he'll visit you himself when the time is right."

Not in good shape? What the hell did that mean? He glanced at his sire and Sweeney, but they had no answers for him. Found in the forest? What forest? Had she been beaten, maimed, attacked? What? How could they not give him more information? Every part of his being tensed as the endless list of possibilities blossomed in his mind.

"Hellfire, I'm not leaving until I see my betrothed with my own eyes. Open the gates!" he shouted.

Her brothers appeared on the curtain wall. "Go away, Drummond," Filib said. "She's alive and 'tis all we can tell you. We have a healer tending her."

Ossian, as antagonistic as ever, shouted, "How do we know you weren't her attacker, Drummond?"

"I was in Edinburgh, but you already knew that. Stop casting suspicion my way when I was nowhere near your land."

"But your clan would be quick to lie for you. We all know that." Ossian spoke loud enough for all to hear him.

MacGruder's second, Struan, appeared on the top of the wall. "Leave it be, Ossian. Anna has already confirmed you were not her attacker, Drummond. But she is in much pain. The MacGruder will visit you on the morrow."

That just wasn't good enough for David. He had to see her to believe she was hale. "I'm sure she's asked for me. Allow me to see her for a moment and I'll leave. I need to know how she fares." He had to know her injuries could be healed. What had happened to cause her pain?

"Nay, she hasn't asked for you. Go home. We'll update you on the morrow." Ossian's harsh voice carried down from the wall.

David wished to argue more, but his sire stopped him. "We'll expect to see your sire on the morrow, lads. Should be enough time to assess the situation and advise her betrothed of her condition. If there's aught we can do in the meantime, please advise us."

Filib nodded. "Fair enough. On the morrow." His voice was barely audible.

David knew he would not get one minute of sleep.

CHAPTER THREE

NOT LONG AFTER ANNA'S FATHER left, the Mac-Gruder healer entered the chamber, bending at the waist as she stepped through the doorway.

"Torra, I'm so glad you could make it. How is your hip?" her mother asked, rushing to the healer's side.

"Och, my joints are always aching, but I must take care of our wee one. How is she?" Anna's mother closed the door behind Torra and ushered the healer to a stool near the bed. The old woman shuffled over, the fingers of both hands bent at odd angles from an unknown ailment. Despite all of her physical complaints, the dear woman's mind was as sharp as ever. She sat down with a grunt, took a few breaths, then began her inquisition. "What happened to you, my dear?"

Anna didn't know how to answer other than to be honest. "I don't know what happened. I recall naught until I awakened alone in the forest."

Torra clucked her tongue a few times as she took in the muddied garments on the floor of the chamber. "Someone must have given you a potion or hit you over the head. Which was it?"

Anna's confusion continued. "My head does not hurt as such…" Her hands reached up to feel for lumps hidden by her hair but found nothing. "But I'm having difficulty thinking clearly. I'm verra tired."

"Potion is most likely." Torra's gaze narrowed on Anna's

face and ran down the length of her body. Anna's mother let out a little sob, and the old healer shifted to look at her. "What is it?"

She cleared her throat and answered, "Anna has some bloodstains on the back of her gown. Lorne fears she may have lost her maidenhead. We were about to get her into the tub. She's a filthy mess."

"Oh dear. Allow me to take a quick look."

Torra asked her to lie down and then spread her legs in a most indecent manner, something that embarrassed her so much she closed her eyes until the healer restored the fabric. "Aye, it seems you could have lost it. I'll not be telling anyone, but you have quite a bit of blood there. Are you sore at all, lass?"

Tears misted her eyes as she nodded. "My bottom feels as if I've been tossed off a horse."

"Your legs are bruised, as well." She patted Anna's hand, something everyone wished to do apparently, then tipped her chin up and whispered, "Did he rape you? Do you remember if he forced himself on you?"

"I don't know what happened." She shook her head, still unable to recall anything about the night. Her entire body trembled at the implications of what Torra had said. She'd lost her maidenhead, and it hadn't been to David. How could she possibly explain this to him, especially when she had no memory of the event?

Her whole body shook as she reached for her mother's hand to help her off the bed, the thought of another man's hands on her making her feel as if there were a thousand bugs under her skin trying to get out. "Bath. I need my bath." Whoever had touched her didn't matter, she had to wash him away, get rid of him before she saw David again.

"That's right. Get her into the tub and wash away the evidence. You need not look at it again. I'll make you a warm draught for you, something to help you sleep, child."

All while she bathed, scrubbing as hard as possible, Torra

and her mother whispered over in the corner. She did her best to ignore them, not wishing to listen to any of their guesses as to what had transpired in the forest. She couldn't consider the full meaning of it—the possible repercussions.

Torra brought over a warm drink and set it on the stool next to the tub. Anna sipped away at it for lack of anything better to do, needing something to occupy her hands, her mind. Her head fell down toward the side of the tub, resting on her shoulder, so she closed her eyes.

A few moments later, she bolted straight up in the water, surprised to see Torra had left the room.

"I remember," she cried, turning to look at her mother. "I do remember, and 'twas not David." She couldn't be more certain. A few brief moments from the night before had returned to her in her sleep—a vague recollection of a man grabbing her and tossing her over a horse, then a clearer glimpse of him as he pulled her off the beast. The long scar traveling from his right ear to his chin gave him a wicked look. Nothing else would come back to her, and part of her was grateful for that.

She squeezed her eyes shut.

"Mama, 'twas not David for certes. I remember the face of the man who did it, and I've never seen him before in my life." Anna climbed out of the tub, frantic, and when her mother wrapped a linen around her, she fell into her arms sobbing.

———◆———

DAVID PACED THE GREAT HALL for the umpteenth time that morn. How his brother could sleep through all this, he didn't know. Daniel was as fond of Anna as they all were, but he was too young to understand how crushing and all-consuming love could be.

"David, you're disturbing my new rushes," his mother reminded him. "I understand your need to pace, but mayhap you could do it in a larger circle."

He sighed, not wishing to upset his mother, but could she not see how upset *he* was? He had no idea what had happened to the woman he loved. His sire came up behind him and clasped his shoulder. "I understand how you're feeling, son…"

"How could you possibly understand how I'm feeling?" He stopped in his tracks, letting the frustration that welled inside him bubble out.

"Because your mother put me through something similar. She ran off to Edinburgh Castle after that fool Baines, and I had no idea where she'd gone. I remember it so well that I think I can conjure up exactly how you're feeling." He put his finger to his lips as if deep in thought. "Helpless yet furious. Lost and anxious. And I'll bet you'd gladly hang yourself upside down from the beams above us if it would settle this problem. How am I doing?"

David had to smile at the image of his sire hanging upside down from a beam in the hall. His mother clucked her tongue. "Och, forgive me, Micheil. I had no idea you cared back then."

His father glanced back at her, his hands still on his hips. "I know. 'Tis a good thing I paid attention to what you were doing, because you surely did not."

And to David's complete surprise, his mother threw her head back and giggled, her long mane of dark red hair loose and full. She had some white strands, but she was still a beautiful woman, and David couldn't help but admire his parents' relationship. He hoped he and Anna would be as happy when they were at their age. In fact, Anna often remarked about how much happier they seemed than her own parents.

His father turned back to him, exasperated. "There is naught worse than the feeling of being powerless, especially when you're in love."

He considered his sire's words for a moment, then said, "Suppose you do know what I'm feeling. Then what would you do?" How he wished he could give him some insight on his problem. "How long must I wait? Can we not return to their land to press for an answer?"

The door to the great hall flew open and Sweeney stood there, out of breath. "They're nearly at our gates, my lord." The words were addressed to Micheil. Even though he was not the laird of the Drummonds, he was still considered of noble status. In addition to being Diana's husband, he was brother to the laird of the Ramsays, Quade, and their other brother, Logan, was a spy for the Scottish Crown. Stories about the three brothers and their children ran rampant throughout the Highlands.

David jerked in response and ran toward the door, his father's voice echoing over his shoulder. "He'll not speak with you until you are behind closed doors."

His sire was probably right, but he couldn't bear to simply stand and wait for the man. He had to see the approaching group with his own eyes. As soon as the door closed behind him, David asked Sweeney, "Who is with him?"

"Both of his sons plus about a dozen guards."

"Are the gates open?" He hurried across the courtyard, doing his best not to appear daft to any of his clanmates. His friend easily kept pace with him.

"Aye. I had the gates opened and sent two guards out to greet them."

David made it to the gates just as the MacGruders arrived. "Greetings, Chief MacGruder." He pointed in one direction. "Our stable lads await you."

"We'll not be coming inside, lad," Lorne MacGruder said, still atop his horse. David had never seen him so drawn and harried. "I'll give you the necessary information here. I care not who overhears us. 'Tis for all to know. They already do on my land."

David couldn't help but stare at the older man's grizzled appearance, something rare for the chieftain. Perhaps he was as concerned for Anna as David was. He glanced at

Sweeney, then motioned for another guard to go to the hall and retrieve his parents. They would wish to hear this.

"No need," MacGruder said. "It saddens me to say this, but my daughter has been compromised. Out of respect for you and yours, I have sent a missive to our king canceling the wedding. My apologies if any accusations were leveled at you. We know you were not the culprit, and I formally release you from your betrothal to my daughter." He nodded his head, then said, "I have naught more to say on the matter. 'Tis a sad day at our castle." He turned his horse around to leave.

"MacGruder, is she hale?" David called after him. "I must know how she fares. Was she hurt?"

The older man turned his horse back, his face showing his pain and fatigue. "She has no lasting physical effects. Emotionally, she is in pain. I ask you to stay away, Drummond. All of you. You will not help this situation by visiting her."

"But I must see her," David shouted for all to hear.

"Do not waste your time coming to my keep. I'll not allow you entrance. 'Tis simple. You are freed from the betrothal. Find yourself another." The slump in the man's shoulders told him much. "I will do what's best for my daughter and my family, so stay away."

David had always considered Lorne MacGruder a strong chieftain. Today, he looked defeated and old. He could only stare after the MacGruders' retreating backs in shock as they moved away from the gates. The betrothal was off without even a discussion. Anna's father had not even given him time to process the news.

His sire appeared next to him. "I caught his last words," he said. "Did I hear correctly? The betrothal is off?"

"Aye." He could think of nothing else to say.

"She's alive?"

"My interpretation is she lost her maidenhead in an attack. He has relieved me of my promise to marry her, but what if I don't care?" He spun around to face his father, suddenly furious at how this had been handled. Anna had been hurt and he wasn't allowed to go to her. To comfort her. To hear about the incident from her own lips. "This is deplorable. I don't accept his decision. I have to talk with her. He has no right to make that decision for us." His voice continued to rise as he watched the distant horses continue their retreat. Everyone within hearing distance had stopped to listen to him.

His mother appeared behind his sire. "David, we will discuss this inside. You are not thinking clearly at the moment. You will tell us exactly what was said, and we'll go from there."

Micheil nodded. "I want you and Sweeney both inside." His gaze scanned the area. "Daniel? Are you out here, son? You're to come inside as well."

At ten and six summers, David's brother had a habit of mimicking his uncle Logan, listening and spying on others. He was quite adept at hiding from view.

"Aye, Papa. I'll be there in a moment."

David barely registered what was happening as his friend led him inside. Before he knew it, he was sitting beside his brother in his mother's solar, across from his mother and father. Sweeney had volunteered to tend the door. He stood beside it but remained within the room. Despite MacGruder's breach of social niceties, this kind of situation was best discussed in private.

"Repeat everything," Micheil instructed from behind the desk. Diana nodded.

David did as he asked, leaving out nothing, then fell silent to give them a moment to absorb the information. When he thought they were ready, he declared, "Whatever has happened, I still wish to marry her."

His mother asked, "Do those of you who were within hearing distance believe what the MacGruder said is true? That the betrothal is being called off because Anna lost her maidenhead?"

Daniel and Sweeney both nodded. Sweeney added, "He was not happy about having to deliver the message."

"I saw him before he came close enough to be seen by the guards at the gates," Daniel added. "He seemed troubled, but not as distraught as he was in front of you."

"What are you suggesting?" Diana asked.

"I'm not sure—" Daniel shrugged his shoulders, "—but it seemed strange to me."

David stored this information in the back of his mind to revisit later.

"And they don't know aught about her attacker?" Micheil asked.

"I don't think so," Sweeney answered, "though the Mac-Gruder did make it clear he knew it wasn't David. He apologized for any implication that he might have been responsible."

Diana asked, "Did he call it an attack? Is it possible Anna was a willing participant?"

"Mama!" David barked. "Anna would not have been willing. She loves me."

"I know, but lassies have been duped before by foolish promises. It was worth inquiring about." She gave his father a sheepish look before shifting her gaze back to him. "Forgive me. You know I adore Anna. I'm trying to think through every possibility."

Silence descended on the group for a moment, and then Diana cleared her throat. "After what you've told me, my suspicion is that Laird MacGruder is giving you the opportunity to step out of your betrothal because he understands the heir to a lairdship would expect to marry an untouched woman. This would change everything in the mind of most Scots."

"But I don't care about that," David said at once. "If she was attacked, calling off her wedding is cruel punishment for something she didn't ask for."

"He didn't mention Anna's thoughts at all?"

"Nay. I have no idea how she feels, but I want to help her. We can move the wedding up. We can marry in a sennight."

Micheil shook his head. "I wouldn't advise that."

"Why not?" Daniel asked, the words he'd uttered catching them all by surprise.

Micheil squirmed in his seat a bit. "Go ahead," Diana said, turning slightly to look at him, "Explain yourself. He's old enough to learn the ways of the world. I'll not coddle him from the truth."

"All right," Micheil said with a nod. "I would recommend waiting two or three moons. She could be carrying this man's bairn. The only way you'll know if it's truly yours is if you wait."

Daniel grew wide-eyed but said naught.

"You are all heartless," David said as he pushed away from the table and began to pace. "If she's carrying, I'll accept the bairn as my own—raise it as my child."

"David," his mother said emphatically, "you cannot."

"Why not?" He stopped his progression, hands on his hips.

"Because you could possibly be tainting the Drummond bloodline. 'Tis your duty, *our* duty, to see that the land is carried through the Drummonds." She placed her hands on the table and stood up. "I know you'll not like it, but I must insist that if you choose to marry her, you will wait until you know for sure whether she is carrying another man's child."

David couldn't believe his ears. His own mother was carrying on as if Anna were a common wench. "She's not a whore, Mother." He was seething with anger.

"I never said she was, but a woman can carry after only one encounter. You must consider the possibility."

His father stood, clearly supporting his mother in her outrageous thinking. "I think she has a good point. You were to marry in a month. Given the circumstances, Anna may not be ready to marry so quickly. We don't know if she's suffered any lasting harm from the attack. I don't trust MacGruder to tell us the truth one way or another. Why push it closer? I find it commendable that you will still take Anna as your bride, but these kinds of questions can bother a man for years. Whether or not you raise the bairn as your own isn't the issue. Someday you'll want to know the truth of the child's paternity. 'Twill be easier if you know the truth from the outset."

His mother added, "And you'll have trouble convincing me that marrying right away is in her best interest. Women have difficulty healing emotionally from such a brutal attack. You have plenty of cousins to ask because they've been through something similar."

David headed toward the door. "I'll be going to MacGruder land first thing on the morrow to ask for Anna's hand in marriage again. In the meantime, see if the two of you can find some compassion."

He slammed the door on the way out, Sweeney doing the same when he exited after him. At least one person was on his side.

CHAPTER FOUR

ANNA SAT NEAR THE HEARTH in the women's solar down the passageway from her chamber. She'd attempted some needlework, but her mind was still in a turmoil. While she could recall the scarred man's face, no other memories had surfaced. She'd seen the blood on her thighs, yet she had no memory of being touched there. Her mother had advised her a long time ago that the first time was painful for a woman, yet she had no pain in *that* place.

Wouldn't she remember such a painful, intimate experience? The thought made her shudder. She pushed the needlework away.

Her father stepped inside, a sad expression on his face.

"Papa? How did it go?" She knew he'd traveled to Drummond land to tell David of what had transpired.

He sat next to her, covering her hand with his. Her mother entered and stood behind him, her gaze cast downward.

"I'm sorry, lass. I told the Drummonds of your horrible circumstances. Asked them how they felt about the marriage. David denounced you. Just as I suspected, he has backed out of the betrothal. I had hoped we would be able to work things out, but he surprised me. He has no tolerance for a bride without her maidenhead."

Anna gasped and bolted out of her seat. "He wouldn't do such a thing. He loves me and I love him. He said naught could keep us apart." Her father's words might as well have delivered an arrow to pierce her heart, the pain was so intense.

"Now, Anna. He is heir to the lairdship. As such, he expects his bride to be untouched. 'Tis the way of all Scots. I do not blame him."

"Then why did you tell him?" Anna shoved at her sire's chest, furious that he had ruined everything for her. The happy future she'd imagined with David—the trips and adventures they'd planned together—would never come to pass. "He never would have discovered it until after we were married."

"You are asking me to lie to the Drummonds?" He stood back, his hands on his hips. "I cannot believe my own daughter would be so deceitful." He turned to her mother. "Jean, did you make this suggestion to her?"

"Nay, she did not," Anna snapped. "I would have told David on my own. I wish you'd never gone! I need to see him. If he has decided he will not have me, he must tell me to my face." She was more than mortified, yet she was still unable to believe David had denounced her. He simply wouldn't do it. Not the man who'd promised to love her forever. She knew him too well to think the visit had unfolded in such a way.

One of the first journeys he'd promised to take her on was deep into the Highlands to Grant Castle, renowned as one of the largest castles in all the Highlands. The Grants had added several wings to the original keep to accommodate their growing family until the additions had surpassed the available space within the curtain wall. They'd had to build upward, making their towers even higher. It was said one could see half the Highlands from the parapets of Grant Castle. The Grants were related to the Ramsays by marriage, so David promised her a warm welcome and a tour of the flowers native to the area.

He'd also promised to take her to Ramsay land, his sire's

clan. He'd told her about his aunt Brenna's herb garden and his cousin Lily's attraction to flowers. She had started her own garden of different floral varieties and it grew larger every year. Her twin daughters loved playing in the dirt and picking the blossoms.

Of course, he'd also promised her a trip to Edinburgh to see the royal gardens. Someday, she'd hoped to have her own gardens behind Drummond Castle.

All her dreams had withered away. If her papa was to be believed, she was doomed to stay here, marooned in Mac-Gruder land. Was that possible?

"Please take me to Drummond land, Papa. I must speak with him in person."

Her father shook his head vehemently, his lips pressed in a firm line. She'd never seen him so adamant about something. "I'll not take you there. Do you not understand that you've been shamed? In fact, you've shamed our name, daughter. Everyone will know why your betrothal has been called off. I'm sorry I must do this, but I forbid you to ever see him again."

She leapt to her feet. "I wish to see him, Papa. If I don't marry David, what is to become of me? Am I to live here forever?" She couldn't stop the racing beat of her heart or the rush of blood to her head.

This could not be happening. Her entire world had just been turned upside down over something she had no memory of at all. If she could see David face to face, she'd convince him to run away with her. They could still marry, they could still…

She raised her hands to rest on either side of her head, as if it could stop the pain or the explosion that was about to take place inside of her. Then she tipped her head back and let out a small scream, wrenching from the bottom of her toes until it tore from her throat, a wail the likes of which she'd never uttered before. "Nay, nay!"

Her sire did not react at all, but her mother had begun

quietly sobbing, dabbing her face with a linen square.

"I'll betroth you to another," her sire said, ignoring both of them. "In fact, I have a couple of men in mind. I plan to visit them on the morrow and discuss the possibility. You can still marry, you are a beautiful woman of a noble bloodline. Someone will accept you."

Her hands clenched into fists. "I don't want another. I want David."

Marry another? Never.

"Stop all of this carrying on. You are a grown woman, not a bairn." His patience with her was clearly failing. The father she'd adored seemed to have disappeared, replaced with an imposter who was doing everything he could to ruin her life. "David does not want you. In time, you'll accept this."

"Never. I wish to see him. I'll go there myself." She pushed past her sire toward the door, but he grasped her arm hard enough to bruise.

"Nay, you'll not leave our castle."

Appalled that he had gripped her so hard, she pinched his fingers. "Nay, nay, nay."

He bellowed and let go. Thinking only of escape, she rushed out the door and hurried down the passageway, only to hear her father's voice behind her. "Ossian! Get her."

Her brother raced up the stairway toward her, Filib fast behind her. Where could she go? Ossian had always been jealous of the attention her sire paid to his only daughter, so he did whatever their father asked, hoping to garner the same attention. She ran, but she knew he was faster, especially on a staircase. When he finally caught up with her, she raged at him, kicking his shins with her boot. He howled but then slapped her, picking her up and tossing her over his shoulder as if she were an animal.

"Put her in her chamber. Filib, go with him. You must hold your sister down while your mother medicates her.

Tie her to the bed if need be."

Anna kicked and pummeled her brother, sobbing in frustration at her own powerlessness. Her brother tossed her onto the bed and sneered in her face. He only uttered one word, but it was the worst possible. "Whore."

She tried to slap him, but he grabbed her hand and pinned her to the bed. Filib held her other hand and said, "Sorry, Anna. Please relax so we can discuss this calmly."

Her mother fussed at the side table, preparing some concoction for her. Her father pinched her nose shut, forcing her mouth open while her mother poured the bitter liquid down her throat. She choked and gagged, doing her best to spit it out, but her efforts were fruitless. Her vision dimmed as the potion began to take effect.

Her memories had already been taken from her once before, and now the people who loved her were subjecting her to the same treatment.

Unable to fight any longer, her hands fell to the bed. She looked at her family and whispered, "Why?" There was no denying she and Ossian had always had their differences, but the others? Why were they tormenting her?

Filib patted her hand and sat on the bed next to her, mopping her tears. "There's naught you can do, Anna. You must let us decide for you."

All she could do was shake her head and whisper, "David."

The last words she heard frightened her more than any other. Her father's voice carried to her. "Jean, if you cannot control her, I'll take her to the abbey. The nuns will handle her. We must do what's best for her."

***

DAVID WAS ON HORSEBACK AT dawn, Sweeney fast behind him. His parents followed at a short distance.

He'd finally gotten his parents to agree on three things. First, and most importantly, he wished to speak with Anna himself. He needed to see she was hale with his own eyes. Was that too much to ask for a couple who'd been betrothed and in love? This was not an arranged marriage but one they had both wanted, a match that had been supported and approved by their king.

Second, he did not consider Anna damaged goods and wished to convince her parents to honor the betrothal.

Finally, they'd all agreed that they would not set a wedding date today. He didn't care about establishing such details. They could work them out later.

He would try reasoning with the MacGruder, but if that failed, he would take extreme measures to make this right again. Anything it took. He hadn't decided exactly what he'd do, but he'd think of something. If he had to denounce his lairdship, he'd do it, though he hadn't yet informed his mother of his intentions.

They were expecting him at the gates and the portcullis was raised immediately. Anna's brothers greeted them and escorted them to the great hall without argument. They left as soon as Anna's parents came down. There was no sign of Anna herself.

As soon as everyone was seated around the hearth, David said, "I'll not take up much of your time. I understand that Anna has lost her maidenhead, and I accept it. I still wish to marry her."

"Son," Lorne MacGruder said. "I commend your strength of character, but do you understand the possible consequences of your actions?"

"I do." He nodded. "We have discussed this at great length. We can adjust our wedding day in whatever way pleases Anna." While he knew that wasn't completely true, he had faith that his parents would cooperate.

"Allow me to give you the exact details of the attack," MacGruder said, leaning back in his chair with his hands folded over his belly.

David listened because he needed to know exactly what his dear Anna had been forced to deal with, but it did not change his mind. When he finished his explanation, David continued on his quest. "I appreciate knowing the circumstances, but none of that changes how I feel about Anna." Though if he were to be honest, the urge to wrap his arms around her and console her this very moment nearly consumed him. He forced his mind to focus on the present.

MacGruder looked at both Diana and Micheil. "It surprises me that you're willing to risk giving your land to a bairn of an indeterminate bloodline. Is this true?"

"Their opinion does not matter, with all due respect. Mine does." It took all of David's remaining control to stay in his seat and not pace the entire hall. His other thought was to bypass this foolishness and run up the staircase to speak with Anna directly.

"You may feel that way, but I'd like to hear it from them. Diana?" He waited for her answer, his gaze boring into her. The bastard knew he was asking too much of her.

His mother always knew what to say. "We accept Anna as our daughter-in-law, whatever comes of it. The timing of the wedding can be decided later, as can the line of descent for the Drummond land. There is no reason to put more pressure on your daughter at such a difficult time."

"Where is Anna?" David asked, no longer able to help himself. "I'd like to speak with her at once."

Her mother answered, "She's asleep. We had to give her herbs to calm her. I don't wish to disturb her today."

"Mayhap this news would calm her, and she would not need to be given potions to put her to sleep," he retorted. What were they doing to her? The more he sat there, the more uncomfortable he became. Something was not right. Something that went far beyond the supposed attack on Anna. The stable lads had been silent as the grave, and the servants had rushed off as soon as the Drummonds arrived in the hall. No one beyond the MacGruder brothers had greeted them.

"David, there's no need for you to talk to her," Mac-

Gruder said.

"I'm not leaving until I speak with her." He strode over to the staircase, only to be stopped by four guards, two guarding the stairs and two behind him.

He chuckled and turned back to MacGruder. "So this is the way you wish to handle this?"

MacGruder never replied.

David shouted, "Anna! Come to the balcony so I can see you."

Nothing.

"Anna?"

"You can yell all you want, Drummond," MacGruder growled out. "She'll not come out. There's no reason for you to return, though you did save me a visit. I've accepted a different betrothal. She's to be married in a fortnight."

"What? To whom?" He stalked back to stand in front of MacGruder. "Did you even tell the person she could be carrying? Have you troubled yourself to discover who attacked her? Why are you keeping so many secrets?"

"Secrets?" MacGruder scoffed as he bolted out of his chair, hands on his hips. "There are no secrets. She's betrothed to Gilroy Walters."

"Walters? He's an old man with four bairns." David threw his arms over his head in exasperation.

"And he's more than happy to marry a beautiful young lass like my daughter. I think this situation is perfect for her. She'll be so busy with the bairns that she'll forget about the tragedy."

David glanced at his parents. "Are you ready to leave? This man is clearly unreasonable."

His mother jumped out of her seat, her expression unreadable. "Thank you for your time, Laird MacGruder."

MacGruder bowed his head to her in return. "Laird Drummond."

Unable to bear the social niceties, David stormed out the door. His only thought was that he had to get away. While he understood his parents had to conduct themselves in certain ways due to their status, he'd hoped they would be more forceful, more opinionated about this looming wedding, this parody of justice. He made it out to the stables well ahead of them. Sweeney, who was waiting just inside the doors, nodded to him and then waved his hand off to the side, indicating there were ears capable of eavesdropping. He could tell by the look on his friends face that he would assist him in any way possible.

He greatly appreciated the man's devotion. If he managed to maintain his status as the next laird of Clan Drummond, Sweeney would indeed become his second in command. A moment later, Sweeney leaned toward him and asked, "Gilroy Walters? 'Tis true?"

He nodded, not wishing to say any more at the moment. He'd have time to explain the situation to him later.

To his surprise, Filib quietly entered the stables. He said nothing to either of them but held his hand out to David as if to give him something. When he reached out to take it, Filib gave him a single piece of parchment. Still silent, he nodded to David and then spun on his heel and left.

David stared down at the small piece in bafflement. He opened the parchment, surprised to find a small pressed flower inside.

Was Filib sending him some kind of message? He showed the flower to Sweeney, whose brow immediately furrowed.

"Something's not right here," Sweeney said in an undertone. "I don't like the way the servants or the guards are acting."

David nodded his agreement. "I was just thinking the same. I may need to go away for a wee bit to settle this, but I want you to stay at home with my parents. Keep an eye on everything that transpires while I'm gone."

"I won't let you down," Sweeney said. "If aught takes place, I'll make you proud."

David had always known Sweeney would be there for

him when he was laird, but he'd little thought he would have need of his friend's skills so soon.

When his parents joined them in the stables, David helped his mother to mount, then led the way back to Drummond land.

He knew better than to speak to them before they were a good distance from the MacGruders' prying ears. Once he felt it safe, he turned to his mother. "You do not believe the fool, do you?"

His mother reined her horse in. "Nay, I do not. Something is afoot, but making the MacGruder angry is not the way to solve this. When we're on our land, we'll come up with a plan."

His sire and Sweeney joined them, their guards holding back in a protective circle around the Drummond laird and her family. His father said, "David, we must act quickly, and mayhap I'll be contacting Uncle Logan. First we head home, then we'll decide what to do."

David nodded and turned his horse toward Drummond land. While he was relieved they agreed there was a problem, they didn't seem to understand his need to act quickly and decisively. How could he convince them that he needed Anna MacGruder in his life as much as he needed the sweet air of the Highlands?

Today's encounter with Lorne MacGruder had reminded him of the man's odd behavior on another occasion—the day David had asked for Anna's hand in marriage. He'd come to the MacGruder keep that day more shaken than a loose leaf hanging from an oak tree during a brutal winter storm. His voice hadn't betrayed him, fortunately, when he'd asked for her hand and pledged to protect her with his life. Even so, MacGruder hadn't given his approval. After giving him a strange look, almost a look of dislike, he'd said, "I understand you'd like an answer now, but I must confer with my dear wife. I promise to give you my answer within a sennight." His smile had been forced, unnatural.

Lorne MacGruder had given his approval several days later, but David had never forgotten his initial reaction.

Aye, something was wrong in the MacGruder keep, and he intended to make it right.

David waited until they were halfway home before stopping his horse and turning to his sire. "Forgive me, but I'll not be returning with you. I'll be back before nightfall, but there is something I must do."

Micheil's face furrowed. "Please promise me you'll not try to sneak back inside the gates by yourself."

He gave his sire a quick nod, then took off toward the horizon. He was going after the one group of people he knew would help him with this situation.

He was going after his Band of Cousins, and his reasoning was the soundest of all.

He'd just recalled where he'd seen that pressed flower before.

It was the first flower he'd ever picked for Anna.

CHAPTER FIVE

A NNA BIT DOWN ON HER brother's hand.
"Ow, you wee bitch," Ossian cried. "You drew blood."

"Then untie me. I heard David call for me. I wish to see him. Please, Ossian. I know you don't like me, but please do me this one favor? Filib?" Her other brother was guarding the door, his face turned away from her. "Untie me. Allow me to speak to him. I beg of you."

Ossian walked away from her, swinging his hand as if to take the sting of her bite away. "Shite, you think you'll always get your way. Always. Well, not this time. Papa's betrothed you to another. I cannot wait to be rid of you at last."

Filib finally turned to look at them. His expression looked torn, mayhap even agonized. He, too, was struggling to cope with the changes in their family. "You don't have to be so cruel, Ossian. Your jealousy of a wee lass doesn't say much about your character. Untie her."

"Shove it up your arse, Filib," Ossian growled. Her eldest brother's edge seemed to have hardened these last days. Though he'd never been kind, she'd never seen him this disagreeable or cruel.

"Hush." Filib pressed his ear to the door, listening to the conversation below stairs. David's voice was so strong and deep that it easily carried up the staircase.

Anna's eyes misted at her good fortune. "He said he still

wishes to marry me. You see? I knew he'd not give up on me." She glanced from one brother to the other, but both of them still ignored her. If David wanted her, why wouldn't they let her go downstairs to see him? Surely her father wouldn't intend to marry her off to another if her betrothed still wished to be with her...

She'd heard her parents discuss the situation earlier but hadn't been able to make out any words.

"Anna?" David's voice for certain.

She drew deep in her belly for all the projection she could muster. "Up here! David, I'm up here." Her voice was not nearly loud enough, for the sleeping potion her mother had started giving her the previous day had siphoned away her strength.

Both brothers spun around and raced to her side, Ossian clamping his hand down on her mouth and growling, "I told you we should have gagged her. You're too soft, Filib."

"Hush," said Filib. "You cannot be heard."

What was happening? Why were they rejecting David's renewed offer?

She closed her eyes, resigned that she would not be able to fight her way free just yet. The important thing was that David loved her. Truly loved her. She could hear it in his voice.

The next thing she heard caused her to bounce up off the bed, flinging her body about in her desperation to free herself from her prison.

Gilroy Walters? Her sire had said he'd betrothed her to an older man with four bairns. She couldn't believe her ears. Didn't her sire care about her at all? Why would he do such a thing? Perhaps her mother had suggested it. She'd always felt sorry for Walters because he'd lost his wife at such a young age.

She opened her mouth to shout for David again, but Ossian's hand clamped down on it. This time, she couldn't fight the tears.

Filib was over near the table straightening things, but he moved over to the door. She heard the door to the outside open and bang shut with a loud slam.

"Can you control her?" Filib asked. "I must leave."

Ossian snorted and said, "Go ahead. She's not going anywhere."

Anna watched her only friend leave. She closed her eyes. She did not wish to see her parents at the moment. Or anyone besides David.

And yet she was driven by something new. David did indeed love her. Getting past Ossian was impossible at the moment, but she'd find a way out later. Drummond land was not that far away.

She'd bide her time and wait until everything was right. All she needed was a horse.

———◆———

THE BAND OF COUSINS ALL came from different parts of the Highlands, but they'd agreed on a central meeting place: Will's grandsire's cottage. Will had hidden there often in his old life as an outlaw. No one had ever found him, so it seemed an appropriate place for the cousins to meet and discuss their special duty to the Crown. Will and Maggie had planned to leave Edinburgh shortly after he did, so he hoped to find them at the cottage.

He made it by mid-afternoon, pleased to see Gavin and Gregor Ramsay working on building a second hut close to the one inhabited by Will's grandsire, Nevin MacLerie. They'd planned to build a meeting place in the middle of their various homes, and this location had seemed to fit the best.

Gavin and Gregor stopped what they were doing to greet him. "I hope you're here to help, David, and not because there's trouble."

Will and Maggie must have heard his approach, for they came scrambling down a path from the top of a knoll, two falcons soaring above them, their wide wing span a pleasure to behold. Though David had seen Will's falcons before, the sight never failed to impress him. "Greetings, David. Will was helping me with the falcons. I almost have Sealgar trusting me enough to land on my arm," Maggie said, her face beaming.

Will motioned for them to settle on a few logs they had arranged around a fire pit behind his grandsire's cottage. "Did you come back to visit?"

David shook his head, still unable to process all that had transpired at MacGruder Castle.

"Then sit. Tell us what's on your mind," Maggie said.

"You know I've been betrothed to Anna MacGruder for a short time."

"Aye," Maggie replied. "Are you not quite fond of each other?"

"Aye," he said, taking a deep breath to calm his racing heart. "We were set to marry in a moon, but the MacGruder has called it off."

Maggie frowned, glancing at her cousins. "Why?"

"Anna was found in a forest early one morning with no memory of how she came to be there. She was lying on the ground when she awakened, a bit beaten up, and had naught with her. When she was found by her sire, she was brought home. Her mother and the healer discovered she'd lost her maidenhead. This is the tale I've been told. I have my doubts about it, but 'tis all I have to go on at the moment." For the first time, his shoulders slumped. The situation seemed so discouraging and hopeless. He couldn't lose Anna, but he wasn't sure what to do, especially now that his relationship with her family had soured like old milk.

Maggie gasped. "Och, who would do such a thing? Steal her maidenhead and leave her alone in the forest, where she could be attacked by a wild animal?

Will nodded in agreement. "We know how serious the

boar attacks can be."

"What bothers me most is they will not allow me to see her." David stood from the log and began to pace the small clearing, picking up stones and tossing them off into the trees, away from the group. When he pictured Anna's father or her brother, Ossian, his throws became more powerful.

"Mayhap she's not recovered yet. How long has it been?" Gavin asked.

"Only two days."

Maggie said, "The other possibility is she's too ashamed to see you. Her lack of memory must be terrifying. Do they know when she left the castle?"

"I know hardly anything. MacGruder is only willing to say that the betrothal has been called off because he does not wish to compromise the Drummond bloodline. I said I wish to marry her anyway, but he claims she's already betrothed to another."

"To whom?" Maggie asked.

"Gilroy Walters."

Gavin and Gregor groaned in unison. Maggie just arched her brow at the duo.

"He's a nice enough man," Gregor said, "but he's way too old for her, and he has several bairns already. They're a bit wild, or so I've heard."

"Aye, I've heard the same," David said wearily. "Probably why he wants another wife. Aught else you can think of?"

"He could be extremely wealthy. Is MacGruder in need of coin?" Will asked.

"If he needs coin my sire would be willing to help him. He would only need ask." He wiped his hand across his face, then scratched the top of his head. Something was badly wrong with the whole situation. "I just don't understand."

The cousins exchanged a look, and Will didn't hesitate to speak for the group. "How can we help?"

David moved over to sit near his cousins again. "I gave

that much thought on my way over. The only idea I can come up with is that Walters may have orchestrated the entire thing to guarantee Anna wouldn't marry me."

"I suppose 'tis possible," Gavin said. "Gregor and I would be glad to visit Walters and see what we can uncover. We can go in disguise as minstrels."

Gregor said, "Gavin's actually pretty good at it." He laughed. "The girls do chase after him when he sings. He has a fine voice."

Gavin just grinned.

"Can you make it by nightfall?" Maggie asked.

David said, "If we don't waste any time, I think 'tis possible."

She shook her head. "You're not going, David. He'll know you."

"I have to come," he insisted. "But I have one more favor to ask."

"What is it? We'll help you in any way we can," Gavin said. They'd all leaned in closer to David as if they knew how eager he was not to be overheard.

"Would you help me sneak into Anna's chamber so I can speak with her?"

Maggie got a huge grin on her face. "Oh, we'd love to help you with that." She glanced at Will, who was nodding his head. "We'll bring you there while Gavin and Gregor go to Walters. You could find out more from Anna than from anyone else."

David smiled, finally satisfied that they had a plan. He still believed that if he could just speak with Anna, he could find out the truth.

CHAPTER SIX

A NNA DIDN'T HAVE TO WAIT long before her
mother and father came up to her chamber.

"Where's Filib?" her sire asked.

"I don't know," Ossian replied. "He left a short time ago.
You did not see him?"

Her father shook his head. "Go find him," he ordered.
Once her brother left, her sire sat down on the edge of the
bed, covering her hand with us.

"Papa, untie me, please."

He reached for her bindings, releasing her hands quickly,
and she kneaded the soreness from her wrists. "Is that better, my sweet?" Her mother sat in a chair near the hearth,
facing the two of them with a nervous look on her face.

"Aye, but I do not understand what is happening. David
was here, I heard him. Why would you not allow me to
speak with him?"

"My dearest, 'tis too late for that. Why torture yourself? I
know you have strong feelings for David, or you think you
do, but that will pass." He gave her a quick smile. "Your
mother and I know what's best for you. You must trust us."

She loved her parents, but it suddenly felt as though they
were strangers. Her parents were much older and more
staid than David's parents, but she'd always believed they
loved her. Quite simply, Ossian was right—in the past, she
had always possessed the ability to convince her sire to do
most anything for her.

Until now.

Until it truly mattered.

"Nay, 'twill not pass. I love David."

Ignoring her comment, her mother moved along to something else. "Have you remembered aught else about the other night? Do you recall anything further about the man with the scar?"

"Nay. I've tried so hard, but there is naught there at all. How could that be? Was I drugged?"

"Stress could easily cause you to forget what happened." Her sire patted her hand to placate her.

"Why can I not marry David?"

Her sire's expression changed, becoming much more serious. "Because David is no longer interested in marrying you. He wishes to have an untouched wife."

"Papa, 'tis a lie," she said unequivocally.

Something changed in her sire's eyes and he grabbed her shoulders and shook her until her teeth chattered together. "How dare you accuse me of lying." The fury in his eyes shocked her. For a moment she feared he'd slap her the same way her brother had, and her hand came up to protect her face.

The sting of her family's unusually rough treatment caused her eyes to water, but she would not back down. "Papa, I heard David say he still wanted to marry me."

"Aye, but his parents do not feel the same way. Lady Diana, the laird of Drummond Castle, is as concerned about bloodlines as anyone. She did not heartily agree. David is talking like a wee lad in love, as you are. 'Tis not the way the world works. You could be carrying some reiver's bairn in your belly. Lady Diana wants an heir of Drummond blood. Nay, the wedding is off." He stood up as if to let her know there would be no more discussion of the matter. "I understand this is a shock for you, but you'll come to terms with it."

He made his way over to the door, then pivoted to stare

at her. "You have no choice in the matter. I have betrothed you to Gilroy Walters, and he will be here on the morrow to meet you. Cry all the tears you wish to today, but on the morrow, you will be kind and accepting of this new marriage. Is that clear, daughter?"

Her head fell back on the pillow. She closed her eyes, knowing it would do her no good to argue with him just yet.

"Answer me, Anna. Is that clear?"

She refused to look at him. "Aye," she lied, "but please keep Ossian away from me. He called me a whore."

Her father snorted and said, "I'll take care of Ossian. Rest up. I'm sorry you've had to go through this, but there's naught that can be done at this point. I'm trying to find a suitable alternative. No lass wishes to live at home all her life. At least you shall have a life of your own full of bairns, yours and his. 'Twill keep your mind from dwelling on what happened."

Her parents stepped out of her chamber without another word.

She rolled onto her side and sobbed her eyes out, but as soon as her parents left, she sat up, determined to get away.

She changed into Filib's breeks and leine, an outfit she'd borrowed from him some time ago to use when riding, then covered it with a gown. Once outside the keep, she'd get rid of the gown and sneak out the back entrance in the curtain wall. It was hidden by thick brush, especially on the outside, but she'd fight her way through it.

Waiting was torturous, but she wouldn't risk leaving early. She asked her maid to give her excuses to her parents—her head hurt and she wouldn't be down for the last meal of the day. Once she heard the sounds of laughter and a few guards in the hall, she opened her door and crept down the passageway toward the back staircase.

Before she moved down the stairs, she listened to see if Ossian was at the table below. His voice was often the loudest, mostly because he imbibed so much ale and loved to brag about his accomplishments. Tonight the laughter was all about the Drummonds. Her family's cruel words brought tears to her eyes, but she swiped them away as fast as they arrived.

Ossian shouted, "David Drummond looked like a drowned puppy when he left, Papa. You need not worry about him taking any action. And his friend was too busy checking out the lassies to help him in any way."

"I wouldn't discount the Drummonds," Filib countered. "David is all muscle and the same size as his sire. You know the reputation of the Ramsays. He could easily bring his uncle here."

"Which one? The old laird can barely move his knee is so bad," Ossian chortled.

"The one known as the beast. Logan Ramsay."

"If he's our biggest threat, I can handle it easily enough," Ossian bragged.

Anna could almost picture him, his chest puffed out. What a fool. He knew nothing of David's Band of Cousins. Nothing of his connection to the Wild Falconer.

When she heard Ossian's voice again, she opened the door and tiptoed down the staircase. She removed her gown and left it on the floor, moving forward in her disguise.

As soon as she slipped the door to the outside open, she peeked around the corner, holding her breath and praying no one was nearby.

Once she thought it was safe, she pulled up the hood on her brat, huddled her shoulders down, and crept steadily toward the curtain wall. Her heart pounded so loudly that she could hear the pulsations in her ears. Her mouth tasted of dust and she did her best to slow her breathing, though it seemed an impossible task.

The door appeared in her sight and she closed her eyes for a moment to say a quick prayer of gratitude. Finally at the wall, she glanced over her shoulder, pleased to see no one there, a sense of satisfaction blooming in her belly.

She opened the door, revealing the overgrown branches and shrubbery, but she was prepared. Using her dagger, she cut away what she could to get outside, ignoring the brambles and sharp edges that cut her tender skin.

When she was finally able to make her way through the dense underbrush, she breathed a sigh of relief and tucked her dagger away, wanting to shout to the world that she was finally free.

Two guards appeared in front of her on horseback. "Heading somewhere, my lady?"

She should have been wise enough to give in to them since she was outnumbered and they were both on horseback, but instead she took off, running as fast as her boots would carry her, heading into the densest parts of the forest where their horses could never make it. The shouts of the guards would draw more reinforcements after her, but she continued in her quest for freedom, closing her eyes whenever a branch hit her in the face.

She hadn't gone far when a body appeared directly in front of her, and she struck him with all the force of her fists.

Ossian.

———— ◆ ————

DAVID STOPPED HIS HORSE IN a clearing not far from MacGruder Castle, motioning for Will and Maggie to do the same. When they drew up next to him, he said, "How do you wish to carry on from here? MacGruder Castle is small, and they only post guards along the curtain wall in the back when word travels about new reivers. There's a section in the middle opposite a thatch of trees. We can climb them to reach the top of the wall, but we'd have to keep an eye out for anyone coming out of the kitchens in the separate building in the back."

"Don't you think they'll have guards posted after the attack on Anna?" Maggie asked.

David grunted his response, "Shite. You're probably right."

Will said with a smirk, "No problem. If there's less than five, Maggie and I can knock them out."

David peered up at him wide-eyed. "Five you can handle?"

"Give or take one," he answered with a shrug. "My pets often help if necessary. They're verra good at distracting the enemy."

"Tell me which chamber is Anna's," Maggie said. "After the three of us climb the wall and take care of the guards, I'll sneak inside to find her. Let her know we're bringing you in. Is there a sister or brother who would help?"

"Stay away from her eldest brother Ossian," David said. "They do not get along. He's tall and thin, balding with a full beard and lighter hair. Her brother Filib might help you. He has a full head of dark hair. A touch of red to it but not as much as Anna's. He came out to the stables earlier to give me one of her flowers, one I'd given to her and she'd pressed. He said naught, but I took it as a sign that things are not as they were presented to us."

Maggie's eyes widened. "For certes, he was attempting to send you some message. Tell me more about him?" She glanced at Will, who nodded in agreement.

"He's the shorter of the two. Far more muscular than Ossian. Ossian looks like he's ready to kill anyone who comes near him, but Filib is more amiable."

Will reached over and wrapped his arm around Maggie's waist. "Return to us as soon as you know whether or not she's in her chamber. If all is as we expect, then David will sneak in and we'll stand guard." He squeezed her to him. "I cannot help myself. I know you can defend yourself, likely better than either of us can, but I'm feeling a wee bit protective of my new wife."

Maggie tipped her head back, and Will dipped his head to give her a quick kiss. The casual intimacy hurt to watch. He was happy for them, but worried for himself and Anna. Would they ever have that?

Maggie smiled and said, "I'll allow it. Is there a back staircase, David?"

"Aye." David carefully explained the layout of the castle and the location of Anna's chamber.

They moved a wee bit closer before dismounting and tying the horses off, hiding them as best they could. Once they reached the wall, Will lifted his wife up to a tree branch, waited for a clear signal from her, and then the two of them climbed up to join her.

"You see?" David asked. "There is naught going on back here."

Will pointed, "Nay, there's one guard over there." He dropped down at once and hit the man in the head with some sort of projectile, causing him to fall to the ground with one swift movement.

Will found his way back to the wall and reached up for his wife. "Go ahead, Maggie," he said. "We'll wait for you behind the kitchens." He pointed to the spot and said, "As soon as 'tis clear, we'll be on our way."

Maggie disappeared as quickly if she were a bee looking for a sweet flower. Anyone who knew her understood that her sting could be powerful. Once she was out of sight, David looked at Will and nodded, grateful to have his cousins' help. How he wished he could pace or practice his sword-fighting skills or something. His body was filled with nervous energy. He said a quick prayer that his love was all right and that Maggie would find her.

He didn't have to wait long for his cousin to reappear. "She's there and most anxious to see you. But there are quite a few guests in the great hall, many of them imbibing. I think it would be a good idea if Will set his falcons soaring over the bailey. 'Twould unsettle everyone a bit, maybe bring them out of the keep."

Will nodded. He clasped David's shoulder and said, "Go. Find out what you can and return. We could try and kidnap her, but she'd have to be fully dressed and ready to go. If she isn't, then we'll come back with more men—Gavin and Gregor can join us at the verra least. Do not do aught that is foolish." He gave him a sheepish grin and tipped his head toward Maggie. "Still, 'tis hard to use reason in such situations. If you bring her back with you, we'll deal with the consequences on the morrow."

David took in his advice, giving a slow nod. Only one thing held him back from stealing Anna away. He'd promised his sire he wouldn't. If he lost their support, where would he take her?

Best if he stopped thinking about that.

As soon as Will called his two falcons and sent them sweeping and diving over the bailey, a large group of men and guards came running to watch the show.

"Go, David," Maggie whispered.

They all heard a loud voice declare, "Is it the Wild Falconer? Is he storming the gates?"

Will's reputation as a vigilante, which had only grown after he was pardoned for saving the king's life, was exactly the distraction they needed. David crept toward the keep and found his way inside, hurrying up the back staircase. The passageway to her chamber was empty and the few torches lining the way did little to fight back the shadows, making it dark, just as he had hoped.

He didn't even bother to knock but stepped inside her chamber and waited for his eyes to adjust to the candlelight.

Unfortunately, there were two people staring at him, and all he could say was, "Shite."

Anna ran to him in her night rail, stumbling in her haste. "David. Oh my heavens, I am so glad to see you."

He caught her before she fell, and he couldn't help but

wrap his arms around her sweet curves. She gave him a quick hug before pulling back and glancing at her brother. "I'm not going to cause trouble," Filib said. "You must know by now that something is not right here. Keep your voices down."

Anna whispered, "Please give us a few moments. 'Tis not fair what has happened. We deserve the chance to say goodbye. Will you not stand in the passageway and bar the door for me?"

Filib gave a low growl, but after a moment of consideration he nodded. "You better do this quickly. I'll not have Papa skin me alive for helping you, though I should be used to it by now." He left the room and closed the door behind him.

David couldn't stop himself. He cupped her cheeks and kissed her, their lips melding together with a familiar heat he'd missed. She parted her lips, tentatively touching her tongue to his with a deep sigh. He'd needed this sweet taste of her. His Anna always tasted of honey and pure sweetness. But he had to end the kiss.

"Sweeting, tell me what's happened. I don't know what to believe. You haven't changed your mind about our marriage, have you?"

"Nay. I don't remember aught about the attack, but Papa says I cannot marry you because I could be carrying a bairn. He said your mother does not wish to risk the Drummond bloodline."

"Och, 'tis not true at all. I will wait for you." He gazed into her beautiful eyes, wishing it was daylight so he could enjoy the richness of the different shades. Their color and depth often bewitched him. If only they had more time, if only he could run his fingers through the silky red strands of her hair, knead the back of her neck to let her know how much he adored her.

"Your sire said he has betrothed you to another. 'Tis true?" He brushed his thumb across the soft skin of her cheek.

"Aye." Her knees buckled and she fell against him. "Gilroy Walters. I don't wish to marry him, but he'll be here on the morrow. I want you, David, only you."

"I'll not allow it. We were meant to be together. You agree?"

She nodded, but then her eyes fluttered shut for a moment. It looked to be a struggle for her to open them again.

"Anna, what's wrong?"

"I tried to sneak away, but I was caught. Papa told Mama to keep giving me a sleeping potion until I marry Gilroy. But Filib spilled half of it on the coverlet just now so he and I could talk for a moment."

"I'll take you away from here. Two of my cousins are waiting outside."

Her knees buckled again and he caught her, scooping her up and depositing her on top of the coverlet. "Anna, can you walk?"

But no sooner had he spoken than her head drifted off to the side. Whatever drug they'd given her had made her lose consciousness. How the hell was he going to get her out of there when she was drugged into a stupor?

The door to the keep banged, signaling the return of several men. Filib opened the door and said, "Hurry. They're coming."

He had to go without her. She wasn't even dressed, had no shoes on. If they tried to make an escape now, it would be disastrous. He kissed her forehead and said, "I love you, Anna. I'll come back for you. I promise." A strange misting in his eyes appeared out of nowhere, something he hadn't felt since his childhood.

Anna opened her eyes for a moment, catching him off guard. "I love you, too," she said. "My sire said he may send me to the abbey if I don't behave and agree to the marriage to Walters."

"Which one?" he pressed.

Her lids fluttered shut and she was asleep again.

"Last chance," Filib said. "Papa just told Ossian to check on Anna."

David ran. There was naught else he could do at the moment. He had no trouble getting down the staircase and out behind the kitchens where Will and Maggie awaited him. With their help, he climbed the curtain wall quickly and headed toward their horses.

Together they galloped back toward Will's grandsire's cottage. They hadn't gone far when they crossed paths with Gavin and Gregor. They continued on at a fast pace until they were certain they were not being followed. Will whistled for his falcons and sent them back into the sky as a distraction. They always hovered near him, and that was usually enough to unsettle any group.

Once the falcons flew off on their mission, Maggie asked, "What did you learn?"

David closed his eyes. "She has no memory of the night of the attack. As I suspected, she wants to be my wife. She has no idea why any of this has happened—and even less desire to marry Walters."

"Why didn't you bring her with you? We'll find you a priest," Will said.

"They've drugged her. She could barely stand up. It wouldn't have been safe for her to leave. She said her mother has instructions to give her potions until she marries Walters. Filib gave her the most recent dose and spilled part of it on the coverlet so she wouldn't be as bad. I have to get her away from there. Gilroy Walters will be there on the morrow to greet her, plan the wedding for a fortnight or two."

Gregor glanced at Gavin, who nodded to him. "Not according to what we learned," he said.

"What do you mean?" Maggie asked, turning her horse around to look at him.

"They're preparing for a celebration. Gilroy Walters is to marry Anna MacGruder in two days when the sun is highest. Then she's returning to his castle to become the mother of his four bairns."

CHAPTER SEVEN

———◆———

IT WAS THE MIDDLE OF the night by the time David made it back to Drummond land. They'd discussed the various alternatives, but ultimately they all agreed that David should go home to speak with his parents before doing anything hasty. He thanked his cousins and promised to keep them updated. His tentative plan was to convince his parents that he and Anna should marry as soon as possible, and if they agreed, he'd lead a group of Drummond guards to storm the MacGruder Castle. The cousins had vowed to join him, but Will and Maggie wanted to search the area first, see what they could learn about Anna's abduction. Gavin and Gregor were headed home to update their clan about David's problems, but they would return with reinforcements, probably Logan Ramsay at the very least.

Convincing his parents would prove to be a challenge. The guards were impeccably trained—some of them had even learned from the Grants—but his mother did not like to send them out unless absolutely necessary. She'd learned caution after the horrific battle that had preceded her father's death. His parents weren't likely to agree with his plan unless he could convince them it was a sound cause without any risk of death to the warriors.

From what David had seen, they should be able to overpower the MacGruder guards with ease.

How he prayed it would not come to that. He hoped Lorne MacGruder would finally see reason if the threat was serious enough.

He left his horse with the stable lad and wiped the sweat from his brow. Holding Anna in his arms again had caused two entirely different feelings to emerge, and they both fought for a paramount position in his thoughts.

Love. His feelings for her hadn't dimmed at all, instead growing stronger every moment they'd spent apart. How he'd missed her sweet voice, her soft curves, her gentle nature. He would do anything to ensure she would laugh again—and often. She had the kind of joy that was contagious. He couldn't help but laugh every time she giggled, which only made her laugh more, causing both of them to explode in revelry.

And fear. Even now, he was terrified he would lose the woman he loved. There was no sound reason for her sire to stop their marriage, and yet he seemed determined to do so.

Why was this happening? This was the question that niggled in the back of his mind. None of it made sense.

Something else was going on, something neither him nor his beloved knew about it. He'd stake his life on it. Unfortunately, he was so distressed over everything that had taken place that he couldn't look at the situation with a clear head. Normally, he was exceptionally good at analyzing problems, but he was too close to the situation to be impartial.

When he stepped inside the great hall, he wasn't surprised to find his sire sitting in front of the hearth, the flames now crackling embers in the dark.

"Papa?"

His sire stood, awaiting an explanation for his late arrival, he was certain. Micheil was still a powerful man, though he'd lost a touch of his strength over the years. "Aye. I'm here." His sire, the man he strove to emulate, ran his hand through his hair to brush the dark strands away from his face. He kept it long, mostly because Diana preferred it untethered and free. "Just wished to make sure all was well, David. Your mother and I are worried about you."

"I'm hale. Have a seat, and I'll apprise you of all that has happened."

His father quirked a brow at him and asked, "Should I awaken your mother?"

"Nay," he waved his hand. "Not yet. Let her rest. I suspect the morrow will be a difficult day."

His father returned to his chair by the hearth, giving David the chance to gather his thoughts—something he always did. He so appreciated that about his father. Uncle Logan would have been shouting by now, eager to know all at once. Sitting in the chair across from his father's, he said, "I went to see Will and Maggie. I needed someone else's point of view, someone uninvolved who could be more objective than you or me."

"And?"

"Gavin and Gregor were still there. They traveled to the Walters' keep to assess the situation there. They discovered that Walters is traveling to MacGruder land on the morrow to meet Anna and marry her within two days."

"And you have accepted this?" The shock on his sire's face was evident.

"Nay, hellfire, nay!" He bolted out of his chair, toppling it over. What was his sire thinking? "She's mine, Papa. I refuse to stand by while her father marries her to Gilroy Walters against her will."

"If both Walters and MacGruder have conspired to make it so, what can you do?"

"Fight for her, Papa. Hell, what happened to you? A moon ago you reminded us all of your story. How Mama fell for that awful knight, Randall Baines, who tricked her into meeting him in Edinburgh Castle. What if you hadn't followed her into the castle? What if Mama had lost her maidenhead to that fool because she was young and naïve or, worse, drugged? Would you have accepted it and walked away and just allowed her to marry him?"

His voice had grown to a bellow that must have awakened his mother. He heard footsteps come down the staircase, and his sire moved over to greet her. Still, he couldn't bring himself to lower his voice. "Is that what you would have wanted Papa to do if you'd been taken advantage of, Mama? I snuck inside the MacGruder Castle tonight, held her in my arms again. Do you know what I discovered? She's so drugged she can barely stand on her own two feet. Should I just walk away? Just say I'm sorry, Anna, but there's naught I can do? I can't believe you would want me to give up on her. You know her, you love her, too, or so I thought."

His mother strode over to stand in front of him. "I would never want you to give up on someone for whom you have such strong feelings. I know your love for her is true, but this must be handled verra carefully. If you and your cousins steal her away in the night, you'll incite a huge clan war. You must be careful, David."

"I'll be careful, but I need help. I'm asking for your assistance. Whatever it takes. I want to make Anna my wife. Will you help me?" David stared at his parents, praying they would not turn him away. "We have to act quickly. Her sire plans to marry her off before we can do aught."

His sire said, "I will support you. I pushed you to see how serious you are about Anna. I'm sorry if that upset you, but I needed to know this was because you love her and not for any other reason."

His mother glanced at his sire, but he couldn't read their unspoken language. They had an uncanny way of reading each other's thoughts. Finally, his mother turned to him and said, "We will support you completely if you can assure me of one thing."

"What?" His arms flew out to his sides as though they had a mind of their own. He couldn't guess what assurance she wanted.

His mother persisted. "Tell me that this is not because of what happened ten summers ago."

His hand went to the back of his head. "You mean with Daniel? What does that have to do with anything?"

"Aye. Promise me that you are not doing this because of what happened that day. You cannot save everyone, David. I know you tried, and I know you carry much guilt over what happened, but 'twas not your fault. Tell me you know that, and it has no bearing on what you wish to do now."

His brother Daniel appeared behind his parents, brushing the sleep from his eyes as he stood on the staircase. Daniel was only ten and six, though he hadn't reached his full height yet, at least his father declared it so. Even in the light of the two torches still burning in the hall, David could see the stump of what used to be his brother's left hand.

David spun around, facing the embers of the fire, tears burning his eyes that caused him more pain than any spark could. Why had his mother felt the need to bring that up today with everything else that was happening?

He had many regrets about that day, but that wasn't why he was going to fight for Anna. He loved her with his whole heart.

He turned back to his mother, not bothering to swipe his tears away. Before he spoke, Daniel came over to stand beside him. "Brother, 'twas not your fault."

He clasped his brother's shoulder and whispered, "I know, Daniel. And to answer your question, Mama, nay. One has naught to do with the other. I wish to save Anna because I love her. Because I couldn't bear to marry anyone else."

Silence fell amidst the crackling of the fire as the family of four shifted on their feet, glancing at one another.

Micheil finally cleared his throat and said, "I would do the same. Diana, 'tis the way I was raised, the way we raised our lads, and the way your sire would want us to raise his grandsons."

She nodded, tears flowing down her cheeks. Her hand came up to brush David's cheek. "We did right naming you after your grandpapa. How I wish you'd both had the chance to know him. You remind me of him more and more every day."

His mother said nothing more, but he could see she fought to control her emotions. Her next comment came out in the barest of whispers. "I cannot believe Lorne would marry his daughter off so quickly after she's been attacked. Has he no heart at all?"

David said, "I cannot even fathom such a thing. I didn't mention it because it will not happen. The thought of her in the hands of another makes me not only angry but ill."

"Which is why I didn't bring it up," his father said. "Mac-Gruder is acting heartless in this matter. We have much to do, but two days gives us plenty of time to act. Agreed, Diana?"

She glanced from her husband to David and then Daniel. "Prepare yourselves. We'll be calling all our warriors to fight tomorrow, and your sire will send missives to his brothers and to the Grants."

"The Grants, Mama? Do you think we'll need them?"

"I prefer to be prepared. They'll not be able to join us right away, but I wish to have them at the ready. What the MacGruder is doing to his daughter is wrong. As another woman, I will stand up for her. We will stand against the abomination of men deciding what's right for women without taking our thoughts into consideration."

"Am I allowed to go?" Daniel asked. "'Tis my right to fight alongside my brother."

David nodded. "I'd like you with me."

"Aye," their sire said. "We need you, Daniel. Get your sword arm ready."

CHAPTER EIGHT

A NNA'S EYES OPENED AND SHE smiled. A distinct aroma teased her, that of David Drummond. He'd smelled of horse with a wee bit of pine mixed in and another fragrance unique to him. She sat up in bed, surprised that her faculties appeared to be back to normal. The sun was rising on a new day.

Would it bring more potions, more lies, more emotional pain?

Or would her knight come for her once again?

Her mother bustled around the chamber, giving instructions to the servants who had carried in the tub and were now dumping buckets of steaming water into it. She threw the covers back and sat up. As soon as she did, her mother spun on her heel to face her.

"Goodness, I'm glad you are awake, my dear. We have so much to do." As she said it, she reached down to smooth her skirts, one of her nervous habits.

"What, Mama?"

"You must bathe. Your sire said your betrothed will be here when the sun is highest. He wishes to meet you, have the midday meal with us. I must help you get ready."

"Mama, please. Who is going to be here today?"

"Why, Gilroy Walters, of course. His blood is not noble, but he will still care for you, protect you, and give you bairns to love." Her mother's voice shook, telling her that her own mother didn't agree with what her sire was proposing—a marriage that would be a farce.

"Mama, I don't want Gilroy Walters. I want David Drummond, and he still wants me, regardless of what transpired during the attack. Why will you not help me?" She had to get her mother to see reason. Why would they marry her to an old man with four young bairns when the love of her life, a future laird, still wished to marry her? Yet her mother seemed more timid than ever of late.

"Your father has made up his mind. This marriage will take place." Tears had welled in her eyes, but her words were unrelenting. She motioned for the servants to leave them alone and then helped Anna out of her night rail and shift. "And please promise me you will not cause more trouble by running away today. Your sire was not happy with your behavior last night."

She wasn't the least bit concerned about her father's happiness, not anymore. "Mama, I will not promise that. If I can find a way out, I will. I have become a prisoner in my own home."

Her mother said nothing but turned away from her to fuss with the clothing she'd removed. She couldn't understand her mother's willingness to go along with this horrid match. While Anna was definitely not resigned to her fate, she decided to let her words sit for a moment. Her sire controlled her mother, without a doubt, and she doubted her mama would willingly cause trouble.

Glancing at the steam rising from the water, she succumbed to the temptation in front of her. The bath was a rare treat, and perhaps it would help further rouse her out of the stupor of the drugs. She slipped into the hot water with a deep sigh.

Her mother quickly scrubbed her back and helped her wash her hair. They didn't speak at all. No attempt was made to drug her. Her sire must have decided she would need to be able to walk on her own or Walters would be suspicious. This gave her the opportunity to think of another possible escape from this mess. If David had only come to her when she was alert, she could have run away with him...

When she finished, her mother assisted her out of the tub and helped her to dress. She wore a spring green gown with a dark green surcoat over it. Her mother did her hair, plaiting it with ribbons interspersed with the delicate strands of her hair.

"Mama, please. Do you not understand how it feels to be in love with a man?" Her whisper carried to her mother behind her. How she wished she could pivot to see her expression.

Her mother sighed, as deep a sigh as she'd ever uttered. "Aye, I do understand, and I wish you could marry your choice of husband. But I also wish you had not been attacked, that you had not lost your maidenhead to a stranger. 'Tis not the way of the nobility, which you know as well as I do. 'Twas a most unfortunate incident, but unless you can remember exactly what happened, we have no choice. This is verra hard on your sire, too. He was desperate when you disappeared."

"How could anyone possibly think Gilroy Walters is what's best for me?" She had to reason with her, make her change her feelings. She'd never be able to convince her father if her mother didn't take her side.

"Once word gets around, your father and I fear no one will have you. Gilroy is willing, so I have to agree with your sire. We must accept his offer before he rescinds it. Better that than spend your life in a tower room." She turned Anna around to face her once she finished with the ribbons. "I want you to have some happiness. My happiness came from having my own bairns. Mayhap you'll feel the same."

A knock sounded on the door and her sire strode inside. Was this her old sire or the new one who didn't seem to care a wee bit about her?

"Are you ready?" he asked. "My patrol has spotted Walters on MacGruder land. He'll be here earlier than expected, in less than an hour." His harsh tone told her more than his words could ever reveal. "You will do as I say and not embarrass me, is that clear, Anna?"

He hadn't changed his mind, and neither would she. She vowed to fight him with her last breath. "Papa, please reconsider this. David said he would have me."

Her father's gaze narrowed at her. "And how would you know aught that David Drummond said? Have you seen him?" As he spoke, Ossian followed him into the room.

"I heard you talking with him in the great hall." She would not admit she'd seen him last night for fear of repercussions, though she'd had no control over his visit.

Ossian said, "I told you, he was here last night. I could sense it. Those falcons swooping around last eve put us all in mind of the Wild Falconer. They say he can conjure up a hundred birds to attack your castle. 'Tis what he did in Edinburgh when Maggie Ramsay was arrested. Now the Falconer and Maggie have married, and David is related to the Ramsays. He was here."

Ossian's sneer must have convinced her sire because he turned to Ossian and then to Anna.

Her sire's hands settled on his hips as his glare bore into her. "Is this true? Was David here last eve?"

"I…I…"

"Answer me!" His bellow made her start. When had she ever seen her sire like this before?

"Papa, why are you treating me like this? I thought you loved me."

Her father pursed his lips and his voice dropped to such a low tone, she could barely understand him. "Answer the question, Anna. Was David Drummond in this chamber last eve?"

She couldn't lie to him, and in truth, she didn't think she should have to. Wasn't it her right to see David? The betrothal had been canceled without their permission. "Aye," she replied, doing her best to swallow the huge lump in her throat.

Her father's hand swung out so fast, she never saw it coming before it caught her cheek with a loud slap. "You will do as I say. Do you understand me? You say *I* have changed? When did *you* become this person who sneaks out at night, who whores around and invites men to her chamber?"

Her mother finally spoke up. "Lorne, please. How could you say something so hurtful to our daughter? She is not to blame for the attack."

"Because…you know why…I will not allow this to happen to me again. Do you hear me?" He spun around to face Anna's mother, his pointed finger shaking with anger.

What was he talking about? She peered at her mother, who blushed a deep shade of red not unlike the skin of a fallen apple. A knock sounded at the door, bringing them all back to more imperative events.

"My laird, Gilroy Walters's guards are at the stable awaiting you to discuss his travel and arrival."

Her father barked, "I'll be right there. Now, Jean, you will have her arranged in front of the hearth so he can greet her when he arrives."

He opened the door to leave, but before he did, he whirled around to speak to her. "Anna, do not ruin this or you will regret it."

Anna had the sudden feeling that the walls were closing in on her, that the floor was about to open up and she would fall into the depths of the darkest dungeon in all of the Highlands. Dizziness engulfed her, but she pinched herself, forcing herself to stay awake and fight whatever effects the potions were having on her. She tripped and fell against the chest, surprised when her hand fell against something—the potion. She tucked it inside her hands and folded them together as she headed out the door.

She would be alert for her David. Some opportunity would come her way, she was certain, and she would not allow it to pass her by. Ignoring her brother, she moved forward, lifting her chin. Her opportunity would come to her soon but staying in her chamber would not help.

Ossian chuckled as if he could read her mind. He held the door for her, and her mother ushered her forward. As soon as Ossian looked away, she rubbed the spot on her cheek where her sire had slapped her. Her father had never raised a hand to her until all this had transpired. How he had changed.

She had to admit that stepping out of her chamber was a relief. Once she made it down the stairs, she glanced around the hall to see who was about. The servants stared at her, dropping their gazes when she passed one of them, none of them speaking to her at all.

What were they thinking of her? Were they ignoring her because she'd been shamed, because she'd been drugged, or because they'd overheard the fight with her sire? At first, she was offended, but then she had a change of heart. If they ignored her, it would be easier to disappear without being noticed. An idea began to brew in her mind.

She didn't know and didn't care what they thought. She just wanted David. Glancing around, she wondered if she could possibly sneak out the back door. "Mama, I think I'll visit Cook, see how she fares."

Her mother didn't deny her, so she made her way out to the building behind the keep, checking the area for any guards. The door to the outside was not far away, but a guard stood on either side of the door.

She waved to them, just to let them know she was aware of their presence, then ducked into the heat of the kitchens. "Cook, what have you for the guards in the back?"

"Here," Cook said, panting from the combined heat of the hearth and the ovens. "These are from yesterday. Give it to them."

Anna smiled and thanked their cook. She hadn't thought it would be this easy. Tucking her hand into the small pocket sewn inside her under gown, she found the bottle of potion that had been left in her chamber. She broke the bread into two pieces and sprinkled the concoction on both, hoping she was putting enough there to work on the two brutes.

The mixture was invisible on the bread, so they had no reason to suspect a trap. As soon as she handed the food over, they scarfed it down with barely a thanks. She waited behind a tree, praying something would happen, and they both fell to the ground in a deep sleep. It had worked! She stepped past them gingerly, approaching the door in the curtain wall. She peeked through it first, fearing Ossian would be waiting on the other side, but he was nowhere to be seen. She stepped through the door and closed it behind her just in time to hear a shout from the keep.

The fallen guards had been seen.

She didn't go far before she was apprehended by two of her sire's guards and dragged back to the keep, though they brought her around to the front. Her sire and Struan awaited her just outside the door. She feared her sire would hit her or tie her to her bed, but instead he said, "Put her in the chair in front of the hearth and don't allow her to move."

Her sire's second grinned and grabbed her by the arm, hauling her toward the door as her father spun away from her and made for the stables.

"Struan, 'tis no reason to hurt me."

Struan glared at her. "Aye, 'tis a good enough reason to me. I am not fond of a lassie who tortures her sire so. 'Tis my job to make his life easier, so making you repent your ways falls on my shoulders." He gave her a push to walk in front of him. "You're lucky you don't get your bottom walloped for the way you're acting. Your sire is doing his best to find you a husband. After what happened, you'll be lucky to find any man who'll have you, especially when you've changed from the sweet, agreeable lass I once knew." He pointed to the hearth and said, "Sit and don't move, or you'll sit with me."

He narrowed his gaze at her and stalked away. What had happened to him? She could say the same about his temperament changing.

She sat in the chair and didn't move, dreading the thought of sitting with Struan.

A few moments later, the front door burst open and Gilroy Walters filled the space, a grin on his face. "Finally, a wife again." He stepped into the hall and said, "And a fine beauty she is."

Her father entered and motioned for her to stand to greet him. She did as he requested and made her way over to Walters, though she did not venture close enough for him to touch her. Struan stood behind her, this man in front of her, and her father a stone's throw away. This was not the predicament she wished to be in at the moment.

She dropped her gaze from Walters's beady eyes. He wasn't bad looking or obese. He still cut a fair figure and dressed well. His brown hair was flecked with gray, and he parted it down the middle a most unusual way. Some might call him handsome or debonair, but not Anna.

His gaze spoke of a man who couldn't wait to bed her, and it made her uncomfortable. He was trying to be nice, but the excitement in his gaze turned her stomach.

The back of her neck bristled as he slowly perused her, his gaze lingering on her chest, causing her cheeks to flame instantly. She did her best to slow the panic that had set her heart to racing, the sweat that dotted her palms at the thought of belonging to this man and having to succumb to a wedding night with him.

Frankly, she'd prefer to vomit.

Once he'd taken his time to study her, he spoke to her sire, allowing her mother to lead her over to a chair by the hearth. Moments later, he stood beside the chair, staring again as he made a small bow to her. "My lady. You do look lovely today. I am sorry for all the tribulations you've been forced to endure of late."

"Thank you," she murmured, avoiding his gaze. Her skin crawled as he set his hand on hers, wrapping his long fingers around her wrist and caressing the underside with his thumb. She jerked her hand away, doing her best to hide the gesture from her sire. That spot was David's, the spot he would kiss tenderly whenever she was sad about their time apart. He would kiss her there and she would giggle and sigh, just what he wanted her to do. And he would always follow the kiss with one question: "Better, my sweet? I'm here now."

Aye, everything David did was better. She closed her eyes to erase the image of Gilroy in front of her. He spoke to her brothers and her father, pleased enough to ignore her as she sat with her hands folded appropriately in her lap, eyes cast downward as was 'proper' for a lady.

But it gave her time to think. She would get away from this man. Somehow, some way, she would find her way back to her love.

To her surprise, the door burst open and two guards marched over to her sire, whispering. She listened and heard the one thing that could make her heart soar.

"The Drummonds have been spotted not far away."

Her sire cracked his knuckles, sighed deeply, and said, "How many and how far?"

One guard, his gaze showing true fear, replied, "Looks to be their full force of warriors."

The second guard pulled on his tunic around his neck. "Aye, the full lot of them are here, and I believe I saw some Ramsay plaids on our last patrol, as well. About an hour away."

Her sire turned to Gilroy Walters and said, "I'll contact you when this is over." Then he turned to Ossian and said,

"Take her back to her chamber."

Ossian yanked her arm and pulled her toward the staircase.

"Here now," Walters said. "There's no reason to mistreat the lass, is there? I'll not care to see my wife covered in bruises."

Perhaps the man deserved a little more credit than she'd given him. He seemed a fair bit kinder than her own family, though he had not directly intervened to help her. A few more words from her father, and he was rushing toward the door to flee.

Another guard came flying in, stopping Walters in his tracks, and said, "They're almost here. There's another contingency to the front, and they're moving at a full gallop."

"I was leaving," Gilroy said, "but perhaps 'twould be better for me to stay. I'd like to know the final decision before I head home."

That was the last she heard of the conversation in the hall. Ossian pinched the tender skin under her arm before he tightened his grip. If she had to guess, her dearest brother enjoyed causing her pain. She kicked and shouted all the way up the staircase while Ossian mauled her and laughed with glee. However much she fought him, he did not slow his pace. Her sire and mother followed her up the staircase, and once they were inside the chamber, her sire said, "Wrap her up in her brat, then mix another potion. I'm putting her in hiding. If the Ramsays join in, there could be trouble. I don't want that Logan Ramsay anywhere near her."

That was the last thing she remembered before she was forced to swallow another potion. She spat and kicked as much as she could, but her sire and brother overpowered her. Every time she managed to spit out the concoction, they just gave her more.

Her eyes closed to visions of Gilroy Walters waiting for her at the chapel.

CHAPTER NINE

———◆———

DAVID RODE IN FRONT FLANKED by his sire on one side and his brother and Sweeney on the other. Two guards rode in line with them, each carrying the Drummond banner. The Scottish breeze across the valley caught the edges of the flags, snapping them with vigor.

The snapping sound made him sit taller in his seat. The pride he felt in leading this fearsome army of Drummond warriors with his father and brother no doubt showed in his expression and his countenance. He set his horse to a healthy canter once the gates of MacGruder Castle came into view.

They had no time to waste.

When they reached the portcullis, he was surprised to see the heavy grille had been raised at their approach. He stopped, indicating with his hand that all were to stop behind him. "I wish to speak with your laird."

The guard standing above him said, "You and your sire and no others."

His father didn't hesitate. "We'll enter with five guards. They may remain in the courtyard, but they'll follow us."

The guard exchanged a glance with one of his fellows. "Accepted. Enter. My laird awaits you in the great hall."

David's gut began to roil, a slow churning that reminded him to keep his temper in check. This was too easy. Something was surely afoot, some underhanded deed being covered up. In fact, he was so certain of it that he motioned for Sweeney and his brother to ride around to the back of the curtain wall while they were inside.

He vowed not to mention that he'd been to see Anna last night, or that he was aware of the appalling way she'd been treated. He dismounted, resting his hand on the hilt of his sword just to remind himself that his weapon would serve him well, if necessary.

As they crossed the bailey, Micheil whispered orders to their guards. The men took up their assigned places while David and his father entered the hall. Once David's eyes adjusted to the dingy interior, they were led to a table in the center of the great hall, where Lorne MacGruder sat across from Gilroy Walters.

"I've come to claim my bride," David said, his chin lifted and his hand on the hilt of his sword.

"*Your* bride?" Walters glanced from MacGruder to David and then back again. "Anna and I are to marry in two days. He has betrothed her to me, said your betrothal is off."

"Nay, it's not. Out betrothal was sanctioned by our king. We were to marry in less than a moon, so you may take your leave, Walters. I've decided to move the ceremony up to a fortnight from now," David said, stepping closer to him with his hand on the hilt of his sword.

Lorne MacGruder stood up, his hand on his sword. "I have rescinded my approval of your marriage to my daughter. I choose to give her to Walters. I've already sent a missive to our king, but you know that, Drummond."

"And what does Anna say about that?" David asked, seething with anger, wanting to reach out and grab the man by the throat. "Or our king? He sanctioned our betrothal. Just because you sent a missive does not mean he will accept it."

"Anna is a lass. I care not what she thinks. 'Tis my job to make decisions for her. And once I advise the king of what happened to my daughter, he'll understand the need for the change and the importance of seeing this done quickly. 'Tis her best interests we all have at heart. Everyone but you, Drummond. You claim to love my daughter, but you're interested only in your personal gain. Anna is distressed and needs to have her life settled. Surely you can understand that after all that has transpired. Anna wishes for happiness. This is her best chance."

Walters nodded. "Agree to this match and go on your way. We need not involve the king in the matter. He's a busy man. Honestly, Drummond, you could have any lass you want. Go choose another."

"I choose Anna. Where is she?"

"She's not here," her father replied, returning to his chair and falling into it with a plunk, a shady grin on his face.

David returned to the doorway to the keep and called three of the Drummond guards inside. "Search the keep for Anna MacGruder." The guards did as they were bid, but he could see that his threat did not bother MacGruder at all. Unable to trust anything the fool said, he headed up the staircase to check her chamber. Empty.

He raced back down the stairs, waiting for his guards to return and report. All three came back empty-handed, shaking their heads.

"Where is she?" David said, feeling his cheeks flush with anger.

"You'll never find her," MacGruder chuckled.

His sire stepped in. "MacGruder, why the animosity against my son? You approved this marriage at one time. He said he did not care if she was untouched, so why have you changed your mind? Are you paying him a huge bag of coin, Walters? If so, 'tis most unethical. My wife sent a missive to our king, and you know how King Alexander favors her. I would advise you to hold off on the marriage for three days until we can determine the king's wishes in this matter."

To David's surprise, Walters paled at the mention of their king, whispering frantically to MacGruder, "You said the king would approve." Lorne's only reply to either man was that same self-satisfied little grin. He had as little care for Gilroy Walters as he had David Drummond. What was at the core of this fiasco?

Walters was unsettled. David's sire had advised him that this man held little land, only had a few families to work his fields. Apparently, he feared having his land stripped from him. He paused, then swallowed. "I will wait, but not more than three days."

"Take your leave, Drummonds. You're no longer welcome here," Lorne said.

"Do I have your word you'll not marry your daughter to Walters until the king passes his decision on this?" Micheil asked.

"Nay, you have no vow from me. You have continued to harass me, and I heard David attempted to speak with Anna last eve. Stay away, Drummond, or I'll see your son's head on a pike in front of my gates."

David trudged back out of the great hall, his sire next to him. Once they gained their horses' backs and circled back to Drummond land, his sire turned his head toward him, speaking only loud enough for him to hear.

"Why is it that you are not more upset about these events?"

David smiled. "Because I asked for help."

"Help? In what way?"

"My cousins have been patrolling the area since this morn. I'm sure they know where Anna is, and I intend to go after her."

His father quirked his brow at him. "Think you they've found her?"

David smiled. "Aye. I'll leave you in a bit and go after them. Then I'll do what I must. If I think we need warriors, I'll return for your assistance." He let out a bird call for his brother and Sweeney. A few moments later they joined up with them. His sire looked at him in shock.

"Where did they go?"

"I sent them to the back of the curtain wall to see if there were any signs of horses leaving that way. Daniel is a hell of a tracker."

Daniel smirked at his sire but then said, "Lots of action a short distance from the back exit, but nothing that went far. All trails led back to the front."

Sweeney added, "Except for yours from the other night. Falcon feathers in one area."

His father looked at the three of them for a long moment and then smiled. "When did you suddenly grow up, David?"

David replied, "She will be mine, Papa. You can count on it."

———◆———

ANNA'S HEAD POUNDED, THE SAME way it had for the past few days. Potions, potions, and more potions. The last thing she recalled was being sent to her chamber after the Drummonds were seen. She forced her eyes open, hoping she'd find David there, but her heart sank when she saw only her mother. They were in some strange chamber she didn't recognize.

"Mama, nay," she moaned, wishing things were different. She pushed herself upright, taking in her surroundings. "Where am I?"

"We're at Lochluin Abbey. Your sire wished for us to take you far away, but the weather did not accommodate it. There are torrential downpours outside, so 'twas safer for us to settle here."

"Why? Why does Papa object to me marrying David? He wants me and I want him, and his parents do not seem to mind at all."

Her mother hung her head, tears misting her eyes until they overflowed and flooded her cheeks. Though her mother was often sad, she'd never seen her this distraught.

"Mama?"

Amidst the hitching of her words, she managed to speak bits and pieces. "My fault…all my fault. So sorry…" She choked out the words, her face cradled in her hands. What could she possibly be referring to?

"How could this be your fault?"

"You don't understand. Run, I will lie for you. Just go. Take your brat and run until you find David, and don't ever come back. I will understand."

Her mother stood, holding her brat up and helping her into it. "I'll cover for you. Just go."

Anna had never been more confused, but though her mother's hitching sobs broke her heart, she didn't intend to squander this opportunity. She gave her a quick hug, then headed out the door. The passageway was empty, but she had no idea which way to go. She headed in one direction but found only the chapel, so she turned around and ran as fast as she could, ecstatic to find the door to the outside. She pushed it open, only to be temporarily slowed by the force of the wind and the rain pelting her face. Taking a deep breath, she plunged out into the storm without another thought, pulling her hood up to protect her face.

Where to go? She briefly considered heading directly toward Drummond land, but the ferocity of the storm changed her mind. Lochluin Abbey was near Cameron land, and David and his parents were allies with Aedan Cameron.

If she could just get to their keep, they would help her.

She ran and ran until the pressure in her lungs forced her to slow down. To her surprise, she hadn't gone very far before she noticed the Cameron keep ahead.

Unfortunately, her luck ran out. The sound of horses' hooves came from behind her, and she found herself scooped up into a pair of arms.

Filib said, "Hang on, or you'll fall off and snap your neck."

Her excitement was only momentary. "Filib, just take me

to the Cameron keep. Hurry."

Another horse approached them from behind, grinding her wishes into the mud. Her sire shouted, "Take her back now, Filib."

Filib turned his horse around and she fell against him, tears mixing with the rain on her cheeks. "*Please.*"

"I cannot go against Papa. I'm sorry."

"Then do me this favor. One favor. Please, I beg you."

"What?"

"Send a message to David. Let him know I'm here." She could see by the clench in her brother's jaw that he was weakening. "Filib, I need your help. Mama told me to run, she knows how wrong this is. Please, I beg you to help me."

He peeked at her face for just a fraction of a second, enough for her to know he did care. He whispered, "I don't know if 'tis possible. Papa watches everything Ossian and I do, just as he does with you."

"What has happened to him? I hardly recognize him anymore."

He shook his head slightly as if to agree with her. "I know not. I don't understand why he suddenly appears to hate David Drummond. But you know how brutal he can be with his warriors. I won't be able to help anyone if he decides I'm his enemy." He gave her a sly wink. "But I know he's wrong, so I'll do what I can."

Once they reached the abbey, her sire bounded off his horse and hurried inside the building without giving them a second glance. Ossian joined them from a different direction. He'd likely been sent out to search for her, too.

Filib helped her down and guided her inside. Many nuns stood in the passageway, their expressions confused and lost. What had happened?

Her brother took her by the hand and led her back to the chamber they'd been given. The closer they came, the clearer the issue became. Her sire was inside the chamber berating her mother for letting her go. She heard a resounding slap just before they entered, and she couldn't help but wonder if her father had struck her mother.

Did his cruelty know no bounds?

Filib stopped her just outside the chamber, holding his finger up to his lips to listen to their conversation.

Her mother said, "I don't understand why you've changed your mind, Lorne. I thought you approved this marriage. What has changed?"

"You and Struan convinced me that the clan could benefit from this match. I believed it would gain me special favor from our king, but he hasn't sent me any coin or offered me more land. He's done naught for me. And neither have the Drummonds. I thought they'd offer to help with our castle. We need a new roof, but they've offered naught."

"They would likely help you if you asked them."

"I'll not do it. I have my pride, and you know how I feel about that family."

"Mayhap the king will gift you something once the marriage takes place, Lorne."

How she wished she could see the expression on her mother's face. Someday, she'd express her gratitude to her mother for standing up for her. And whatever could her father mean? Why would he hold a grudge against the Drummonds?

"We'll never know. Now I know I can't allow this marriage to take place. I never should have agreed in the first place. With the attack, it makes my decision easy. She's tainted, so we'll marry her to Walters. There'll be no more discussion about it."

Filib gave her a nudge, which she immediately understood. The conversation had ended, and he didn't wish to get caught eavesdropping. When she stepped into the doorway, her father whirled around. Pointing an accusatory finger at her, he said, "You will stay here. Understand that I have a decree that I will not bend on. I promise you that you will not get your way, nor will your mother get hers. If you force my hand, I will drug you, tie you up, whatever it takes—and the king will go along with me. I will explain *all* the circumstances to him, and when he knows the truth, he will support me." He cast a scathing glance at Anna's mother, who once again burst into tears. "Your mother understands what I say is true.

"I've been foolish. The Drummonds' attempts to change my mind will never work. I have waited long enough. This stops now. I will invite the king here to bear witness."

She stared at the man in front of her, a man she'd once adored, a man who had been taken over by some unknown force, some sickness, that had turned him so resolutely against her. "Papa, please. I love him."

Her words did not affect him one wee bit, instead making his resolve more forceful.

"There will be no David Drummond in this family."

CHAPTER TEN

DAVID FELT MORE CONFIDENT SIMPLY because Gilroy Walters had appeared shaken by the news that he hadn't given up on the betrothal. But there was no denying that he was a bit shaken himself. Anna was missing, and she could have been taken anywhere. All he could do was have faith in his cousins, in his betrothed, and in their love for each other.

After riding around for a while, he finally found Maggie and Will. The sky had opened in a driving downpour, however, and though he was eager to hear their news, the poor weather made it difficult to hear. Through hand signals they agreed to return to the Drummond keep.

By the time they arrived, Gavin and Gregor were already there with Gavin's sire, Logan. His father and his uncle had always been close, and the two were talking animatedly.

David gave them a cursory greeting and suggested that they all head to his sire's solar to discuss the latest news from MacGruder.

His sire clapped him on the back. "Your mother hasn't left for Edinburgh yet, but I'll find her and fill her in on what's happened. We'll join you shortly." He motioned for Logan to follow him.

Once the group had settled inside the solar, David behind his sire's desk and his cousins seated around it, a knock landed on the door. Daniel stuck his head inside. "May I join you?"

David glanced at Maggie and Will, the uncontested leaders of the Band of Cousins. Both of them nodded.

The cousins greeted Daniel, but they quickly turned their attention to David.

"Tell us everything," Gregor said.

"There isn't much to say other than I could use your help. Our betrothal was canceled because Anna was attacked, something she can barely remember. Her sire claims she lost her maidenhead, which he's used as grounds to call off our wedding and promise her to another, Gilroy Walters. As some of you know, I did sneak in to speak with Anna last night, thanks to Will and Maggie's help, and she is not interested in marrying Walters. She belongs to me, even if she lost her maidenhead. I will accept her child as my own should it come to that. Mama intends to speak with the king about the situation."

"When is the marriage set?" Maggie asked.

"MacGruder planned to marry them in two days, though Walters agreed to wait until the king gives his approval."

"So how can we help?" Will asked. "Is this not up to the king?"

There was a sinking feeling in David's stomach. Until that very moment, he'd still hoped Will and Maggie might have seen the Drummond guards spirit her away.

"Anna has disappeared," he said, keeping his voice even. "She was nowhere to be found in the keep, and MacGruder will not reveal her location. He's scheming something, and I would like your assistance in locating her."

Another knock on the door interrupted them, and David's parents stepped inside along with Uncle Logan.

"Mama? I thought you were heading to Edinburgh." David stood from behind the desk and offered his mother the laird's seat.

She sat down. "I found I could not leave without knowing how it went with the MacGruders. I'm pleased there was no need for a battle, but 'tis troubling that Anna is missing."

"Aye, I don't trust her sire at all. I have this niggling feeling I need to find her, or he'll marry her to Walters as soon as possible. What do you think?"

His sire leaned against the wall, folding his arms in front of him in a way that reminded him of Uncle Logan. "I don't think Walters will agree without the king's approval. He stands to lose everything. I'm surprised MacGruder is willing to risk so much. There is definitely something driving this sudden change in his behavior, but I haven't a clue what 'tis."

Diana shook her head. "Micheil, remember he's not always of sound mind. Do you recall the story of how he sent all his servants away and hired new ones? It happened before we were wed. He's had episodes of being unstable."

"You bring up a valid point, Diana. The man can go into uncontrollable rages. What if the king were to come instead of just sending his decision? Think you MacGruder will calm down if the king himself intervenes?"

Uncle Logan said, "The only reason the king would come is if he believes MacGruder does not intend to honor the betrothal. King Alexander will not go against Diana and Micheil's wishes. Still, he may send a number of guards to make certain his will is upheld. That could be the only way MacGruder will see it done."

"I'm not waiting," David insisted. "I'm going after her, but I could use your assistance in determining where to find her. The only possibility I can think of is that she mentioned he'd threatened to bring her to an abbey if she didn't fall into line and marry Walters."

Gavin gave him a cat-like grin, then waggled his eyebrows at him. "As it happens, Gregor and I noticed some unusual happenings at Lochluin Abbey. Papa wished to visit with Aedan and Jennie this morn, so we made a short jaunt out to see them. Unfortunately, they are visiting the Grants at the moment. We did ask his guards if they'd seen aught unusual, and they said nothing appeared to be amiss on their land. But when we took our leave, we noticed some horses and a cart hidden near the abbey. At the time, we had no idea who it could be, but mayhap 'twas Anna?"

David's hopes soared. Finally there was news of something that could help them out. She'd mentioned the abbey. It had to be Anna. Her sire sent her there, now he was certain.

Uncle Logan said, "I didn't see any extra guards. Would MacGruder risk leaving her there unguarded?"

David's sire rubbed his chin. "Possibly. Mayhap he's keeping his guards at his castle for fear of an outright attack. We were there with most of our guards early this morn. Or it could be that he no one would dare take her form the abbey."

"Then that's where I'm headed," David said eagerly. "At least 'tis a start. Rather than have everyone go with me, I would prefer we split up, see what's happening elsewhere in case I'm wrong."

Gavin nodded. "We'll go back to Walters's estate, see what the word is there."

Diana said, "I know you wish to hurry, David, but the weather is horrible right now. It'll be nightfall if you leave now, and traveling in a storm at night is dangerous. I'd prefer you wait until the rains slow, otherwise you could be caught in mudslides. That goes for all of you. I'll go to the kitchens and have them fill a table in the hall with food and drinks. You'll need sustenance before you set out." She stood up and smiled at the group. "Oh, how I wish my dear papa was here to see you all. He would be so proud."

She left the room with a swish of her skirts, Micheil behind her.

David said, "Did anyone learn aught else?"

Will cleared his throat. "We traveled through some unsavory neighborhoods of Edinburgh and claimed to be looking for the man with the scarred face. He is known, but we weren't given a name. It sounded possible he might be connected with the network of men who sell bairns across the water."

Maggie nodded. "As you all know, we've been searching for more information about the network for nearly a month, but no one has given us any names or even locations. The best information we've found is that the network constantly changes. They don't keep the lasses in the same places all the time."

"Then how will we find them?" David asked.

Will said, "We've come to the conclusion that we need to find more victims who can assist us. The only solution we can think of is to try to be at the firth when the exchange is made, but many ships come into port every week."

"There must be some way to track legitimate shipments."

"Aye," Will said, "and we may be forced to do that. We'll need the entire Band of Cousins to help us if we find ourselves going after a large ship that has men on the ground making an exchange. We were lucky when we found Baines in Edinburgh, but we never stopped the ship, so I'm sure the merchant is still doing business with someone. Where there's money, criminals abound."

They all sat silently for a moment, thinking on the problem, when the door opened and Micheil announced, "Meat pies and cheese for all."

David waved the others on, pulling Will and Maggie back at the last moment. "I'm going to the abbey now. In this weather, 'twill be nightfall before I get there. I'm going up to my chamber and down the back staircase. Don't let on what you know."

"And if she is there?" Maggie asked.

"I'll steal her away. 'Twill be easier if there isn't a big group with me."

"Aye, but you'll need protection," Will said. "We're going with you." Maggie nodded her agreement, chewing on her bottom lip.

"What can we tell your parents?" Maggie asked.

Will said, "If David goes to his chamber, he'll be gone before they ever check on him. You and I will take our leave a short time afterward. We'll say we're going to rub our horses down."

"That should work. Uncle Micheil will figure it out eventually, but you should be well ahead of him. We'll meet near the abbey?" Maggie asked.

"Aye," David replied, a spark of hope blossoming inside him. "It's a sound plan. A small lead is all I'll need."

"Leave your horse in the copse of trees near Uncle Aedan's hill in the back. Then we'll know you're still there." The three agreed on the plan.

Maggie gave David a quick hug before they left the solar. "We'll help you get through this, cousin, and then we'll look into what really happened to Anna."

David waved at the dais as he stepped into the great hall. "I'm in need of a change of clothing." It helped that he was drenched from the heavy rain. He took the stairs two at a time and headed to his chamber. Will and Maggie, bless them, had started to tell the others an animated story about Will's falcons. They were covering for him, and he'd use the time as best he could.

Tossing his Drummond plaid to the side, he put on the black tunic and black and white plaid he and the Band of Cousins had adopted as their disguise for undercover work, grabbed his brat, and then hurried down the back staircase. It rained so hard that the stable lads weren't about when he saddled his horse and left. Fortunately, he hadn't seen anyone who would question his attire, which was mostly hidden beneath his brat.

He rode as hard as he could for Lochluin Abbey, eager to see his love again and assure himself she was hale. By the time he arrived, the rain had slowed. He left his horse in the copse of trees as discussed with Maggie and Will. He was almost out of the area when he heard approaching hoofbeats, so he hid to see who it was.

His first impression of the rider was of a tall, braw man, and then recognition set in. He couldn't have been more shocked. "Daniel? What the hell are you doing here?"

His brother said, "I came to protect you. What they're doing is wrong."

"But Mama and Papa will have my arse for this." He had to admit he was surprised at Daniel's gumption. Daniel would always be his little brother, which had blinded him to the man he had become. Many times he'd tried to protect him because of his injury.

He'd been wrong to discount him.

"You know how Mama and Papa hate it when you sneak away."

Daniel pursed his lips. "I know, but I've been sneaking away my entire life, have I not?"

"Aye. You did it most when you were three or four summers."

"I don't recall that, but I know I did it many times before the accident. Should I stop being myself because I lost my hand?"

"Nay," David said, clasping his brother's shoulder. "You should not let the injury ruin your life."

"If I did, the injury would win, and I refuse to let that happen. Besides," he said with a smirk. "Don't you know they'll never miss me? They still think me too young for everything, just as you do. I'm here to prove you all wrong."

"Guilty, I admit it," he clasped his brother's shoulder and said, "You're welcome to assist me. Lochluin Abbey is quite large and there are two separate buildings. It could take me a long time to go through both. I have no idea where she is. I also have no idea how many guards MacGruder brought, though I haven't seen many yet. They must be posted inside."

"It's possible she's not here," Daniel reminded him.

Aye, but he didn't want to accept that.

Daniel broke into his thoughts, forcing him to move and not dwell on the unknown as he oft did. "Allow me to search one building while you check the other." He crossed his arms, acting as if he had no disability at all from losing his hand to a sword. Perhaps it was time for David to start treating him the same way.

"All right. You can search the monk's building, and I will focus on the main abbey. I expect to find her within the nun's quarters. If you do not find her, meet me back here. Will and Maggie plan to meet us here."

They agreed and then headed toward the abbey.

He was proud of his brother. Though he'd told his mother the truth the previous night—he was not driven by the urge to save everyone but rather by his love for Anna—he'd never forget the day Daniel had lost his hand.

His brother had been only six summers, and he'd been nine. Daniel had snuck away from the keep with one of his friends to swim in the loch. When his absence was discovered, David rode his horse straight to the loch, hoping to find him there and get him home before there was too much fuss.

When he arrived, he came upon a melee.

That moment would haunt him forever.

Two reivers were taunting the lads, strictly for their own entertainment, or so it appeared. One man was holding Daniel's friend underwater in the loch, and Daniel had his small sword drawn and was doing his best to fend off the other one. Though the reiver who taunted Daniel had his own sword drawn, he hadn't started swinging. He was teasing the lad instead.

David saw only saw two choices in the moment: help Daniel or help his friend in the water.

He jumped down from his horse and pulled his own sword out and headed straight for the man who held the lad under the water in the loch. He swung his blade and caught the reiver in the back of his head with the flat of his sword, intending to make him stop. He caught him hard enough that he had to let the lad go.

The poor boy's head popped up out of the water, gasping for air, but he was able to scramble back toward the edge to get away from the beast who was now struggling to keep his head up.

David turned back to Daniel and ran toward him. In that instant, barreling with his sword arm raised as any nine-year-old lad would, something unimaginable happened. The second reiver swung at Daniel's small sword and sliced his hand off in one clean stroke.

Daniel's screams practically deafened David. He lunged at the disbelieving reiver, who looked stunned as he watched the lad's blood pulse out of his body. David drove his sword straight into the bastard's belly, then let go of his sword to grab Daniel.

He didn't know what to do, but he recalled watching Aunt Brenna, the healer, tie a tourniquet around someone's arm to quell the bleeding of a deep wound, so he tore strips off his plaid and wrapped them as tightly as he could around Daniel's arm.

His brother lay on the ground and screamed in pain. His friend had come along, taken one look and fainted, while the other reiver had already recovered enough to run off. David understood why when he saw the cavalry of horses heading toward them, his sire in front.

Anxious to get to them, he threw Daniel on his horse and climbed up behind him. As soon as his brother was settled in front of him, he set off toward the men at a gallop, pushing against the bloody stump to try to stem the bleeding.

Daniel looked pale and had stopped screaming, an indication of how shocked he was about the entire event, and that he was weakening from all the blood he'd lost. He huddled against his brother for support.

When they reached Micheil's horse, David slowed enough to say, "His friend fainted and he's still there. Papa, Daniel's hand, he lost his hand."

Their sire turned pale, but he recovered enough to say, "Ride on as fast as the horse will carry you. I'm behind you." He bellowed various instructions at the rest of the guards, some to get the healer, some to fetch the other lad, and the remainder to search out any lingering reivers.

The Drummond healer tended Daniel immediately, closing the bleeding vessels. Aunt Brenna and her sister, Jennie, both wonderful healers, arrived the next day. Daniel had lost a great deal of blood, and he didn't move out of bed for days, but he'd survived.

Ever since that day, David had regretted not going to save his brother first.

His parents never said it.

Daniel never said it.

But he told himself every day that he could have done better. No matter that the other lad had appeared to be in greater danger and had probably only survived because of David's efforts. No matter that Daniel and his friend shouldn't have been out there without any guards, or that Daniel himself could have gone for help.

He'd always feel guilty.

He still considered it his greatest failure.

And while he wanted to save Anna because she was Anna, his love and his future wife, he also wasn't sure he could bear it if he failed someone he loved for a second time.

He couldn't let it happen.

CHAPTER ELEVEN

DAVID LED HIS BROTHER OVER to the monk's building, then nodded to him as he turned around to sneak into the back of the abbey.

He was able to find a door leading directly into the cellars. The abbey was situated amidst rolling hills and the back was at the lowest point. This area hadn't experienced a direct threat for many years, for it was well known that the abbey's wealth was under lock and key. That, plus the Scots' belief that the church and everything inside it was sacred, saved them from frequent attacks.

He crept down the passageway, amazed at the peace and quiet he found within the abbey. But the quiet fooled him. He stepped around the next corner and ran directly into Filib standing in the middle of the passageway. There was no one else about, since they were in the chapel. Mayhap it was time for worship. He wasn't going to let Filib stop him, but he thought it possible Anna's brother would be willing to help her again, just like he'd done at the MacGruder keep.

"Is Anna here?" he asked Filib.

Filip put his finger to his lips, motioning for him to lower his voice.

"Aye, she's here. My sire has gone off with Ossian, and Mother is in a separate chamber." He ran a hand through his hair. "Anna tried running off to Cameron land, but I brought her back. 'Twas on my sire's orders, but I know 'twas wrong."

"Allow me to speak with her, please. Give me an hour with her. We deserve that much."

Filib rubbed his forehead, deep in thought, and then finally nodded. "Wait here. I'll bring her to you."

"My thanks. I'll be right here." He placed his sword back in its scabbard and turned around to make sure he was alone. Filib hurried to the end of the passageway and disappeared through a doorway, likely to a stairwell. The place was so quiet, he wasn't worried about running into anyone down here. Pacing back and forth, he did his best to formulate a plan, but his mind was too jumbled. In fact, his thoughts were so far away that he didn't notice the small figure coming toward him until she was almost upon him.

When he heard her approach, he jerked his head up, shocked he'd been caught unaware, but his surprise turned to joy as Anna came running down the passageway toward him. She threw her arms around his neck with a wee hitch in her breath.

He tugged her close, tucking his head low enough to take in her sweet scent, so grateful to have her in his arms once more. He could feel her body shaking from tears, but she still clutched him with a grip that said she'd never willingly let go, her body melding to his in a familiar way.

"Oh, David. I'm so happy to see you." Her voice hitched between her tears. "I've been so frightened. My sire has turned daft for certes."

"Hush," he whispered, pulling away to kiss the top of her head, her forehead, and the tears that covered her cheeks. "I'm never letting you go. Never."

She managed to stop her tears enough to step back to gaze into his eyes. "What are we to do? I'm so worried."

"I'm taking you away from here." His lips settled on hers and she parted for him with a sigh, the warmth and taste of her reminding him of their love. How he wished to make her his right now, but surely it would be wrong to do such a thing in an abbey.

When his mind finally rejected the tantalizing thought, he pulled back and said, "I'll have my cousins find a priest and we'll marry in Drummond Hall on the morrow. Find your cloak because the weather is brutal, but I'll get you away."

Anna took his hand and led him to an empty chamber down the passageway.

"Where is Filib?"

"He said he had something to do and would return in an hour. Mama is asleep in our chamber above stairs. I snuck out when Filib told me you were here." She closed the door and turned to him. "Please listen to me." Her hands reached up and cupped his cheeks, an urgency in her eyes that he didn't understand. "I'm begging you not to take me away yet. Make me yours. I wish to give my body to you, even though I do not have my maidenhead."

"Anna, nay. 'Tis wrong. We are not married, but trust me that we *will* be married." How he'd love nothing more than to do what she asked. At this moment, she reminded him of the lass who had pushed him into an alcove just to kiss him not so long ago. How his love had grown since then. Here she was saying the words that he was thinking. But in an abbey?

"Nay, we will not. I will not marry you if you do not make me yours this verra moment."

David's eyes widened. "You do not mean that. You're frightened and confused. You will be my wife first."

"Nay. My father means to see this through, and I don't wish to become Gilroy Walters's wife. If we step outside, he'll find us and take me away from you. I have tried to escape three times and they've always caught me. He and my brother and Struan headed back to MacGruder land a while ago, and they plan to return with more guards. This could be our only chance. He probably has Walters's men watching the abbey. The only place we are safe is right here, right now, and I'm tired of being told what to do. This is my choice, not my father's or my mother's but *mine*. I want you now. Everything in my life has been in a month, on the morrow, or in two days. I no longer accept it."

She took a deep breath and whispered, "Now. This is for me, for us. I'm begging you to show me how much you love me, because the thought of never knowing that frightens me more than whatever my father could do. Please make love to me, David. Please claim me as your own."

One tear fell onto her cheek and he was lost. He placed his lips on the streak of dampness left behind by the falling drop. He tasted the saltiness of her sadness and kissed a trail over to her lips. She opened for him, parting her lips with a sigh as his tongue met hers and they dueled a dance that went straight to his cock.

She was in a night rail, so he could feel her soft breasts pressed against his chest. He stood back and removed his brat before lifting her and settling her on the small pallet. "My sweet, I would love to do this properly and spend hours loving your body, but we don't have that kind of time. My parents and my cousins will follow me here. I'll do this but understand that you are already mine in truth."

"Please, David. I need to feel our love beyond the taste of your lips. This is right and true. I love you with all my heart, my body, and my soul. Love me, even if it can only be for a few minutes."

"Aye, I will, but hear me now, I'll never let them take you away from me. Never. This is as sacred as a handfasting to me."

He kissed her softly, teasing her, angling his mouth over hers so he could go deeper, tangling his tongue with hers while he moved her chemise up so he could cup her breasts, caressing each one with the softest of touches, tweaking her nipples until they peaked and she squirmed beneath him. How long had he dreamed of this moment?

He did his best to slow himself down, to show her how much he cared, how much this meant to him.

"You like this, my sweet Anna?"

"Aye, more please."

"You are as beautiful as the morning dew on the brightest of flowers, sweeting."

She smiled at him. He didn't know how else to tell her she was the most beautiful sight he'd ever seen. He gazed into her eyes, her lids heavy, her pleasure mounting almost at a faster pace than his own. How he wished he had the time to watch her as he taught her the pleasure he could give her. He moved down to kiss the valley between her breasts. "You are lovely, your heart, your skin, everything about you." He kissed a slow trail around both mounds before taking one breast full in his mouth, suckling her and laving her until she cried out.

"David!"

He preened with pride. "Hush, sweeting." He reached down to the vee between her legs, teasing her until she parted her thighs for him. Pleased to find her hot and slick, he rubbed her nub with his thumb while he moved his finger inside. She moaned and opened her eyes to stare at him, her hooded gaze full of confusion and a trust that humbled him. He settled between her legs, teasing her entrance to prepare her for him. "If this hurts, you tell me."

"I will. Do this, please."

David slid into her, allowing her juices to ease his entrance, but then he stopped. Since he'd never taken a virgin before, he didn't know what to make of what he'd found.

But it was impossible, wasn't it?

"Anna, I cannot go any further."

———◆———

LORNE MACGRUDER CLOSED HIS SOLAR door to be certain they would not be overheard. He took a seat behind his desk and pointed to two chairs for Ossian and Struan.

"I want this ended." Then he pointed to Ossian. "I've told you if I'm unhappy, I'll switch things around again. You need to make me happy or I'll carry out my threat. Anna and David Drummond *cannot* marry, 'tis that simple. Do not question my motives. I want her married to Walters as soon as possible. I've only returned here to make sure the Drummonds haven't planned a full-scale attack."

Ossian said, "You shouldn't have left her alone. I told you I would have gladly stayed."

His father replied, "Your talents would be wasted inside the abbey. I need you to stay close to protect me. I don't trust the Drummonds not to attack in the middle of the night."

Struan shook his head. "No Scot would risk violating the sanctity of the abbey. If she were outside, then I'd worry. We left a few guards, they should be enough."

"There may be others besides the Drummonds coming for us and you know it," Lorne stated. Couldn't they see what was brewing? Everything had started to go wrong when Anna, the foolish girl, had fallen for David Drummond. He hated the Drummonds. He'd only gone along with the entire fiasco in the hopes of getting something out of it. However, it hadn't taken him long to realize his mistake. Someone like David Drummond could uncover everything if he was allowed to come and go as he pleased from the MacGruder keep. Even Struan had noticed the way the lad kept asking questions, how he refused to let go of anything. He would not have some foolish lad risk everything he'd worked so hard to keep secret. Things had to stay the way he'd planned.

Struan understood how the littlest things could ruin all your plans.

"Who else would come?" Ossian asked, a bit of a gleam in his eyes.

"The Ramsays are probably on their way. Logan Ramsay, that bastard, is likely watching us as we speak. He's always where you least expect him to be, watching whatever you're doing. I tried to have my men steal a few cattle from the Menzies, but who showed up as surely as if we had invited him? Logan Ramsay. I cannot tell you how often that has happened in the last two decades."

A knock sounded on the door of the great hall, so Struan left to answer it.

Lorne whispered, "No one else knows but us. Stop panicking. I told you I'd take care of it and I will. But you need to do what I tell you. This has to happen my way."

Ossian said, "I will not lose what you've promised me. I care not what it takes. Whatever you ask, I'll do it. 'Tis too important to me. I'll not lose it."

There was a fury in his boy's eyes unlike anything he'd ever seen. "I'll protect you, Ossian. You are my heir."

Struan stepped back inside. "We may have more work to do."

"Why? Who was at the door?"

"One of the guards on patrol. There are more warriors headed this way."

Ossian's eyes widened, a smirk crossing his face as if the prospect of battle excited him. "Ramsays?"

Lorne nodded and motioned his hand to dismiss Ossian, who quickly raced out the door.

"Nay, worse," Struan said, swallowing hard.

"Who could be worse than the Ramsays?" Lorne asked. "Remember that Ossian does not know the truth, but I need to keep him doing as I tell him without question."

Struan settled his hands on his hips as he paced. "I don't think you need to worry about that. Ossian will do whatever you tell him without question."

Lorne asked, "Who has been seen heading in our direction? I need to know."

Struan fell into a chair. "Red and green plaids. They're

still a day away, but we must be prepared." He whispered his next sentence as if he was afraid to speak it aloud. "The Grants are coming."

———•———

"I DON'T UNDERSTAND, DAVID. I TRUST you. Just go ahead." Her fingers threaded in the hair at the back of his neck. How she adored him.

"I've never had relations with a virgin, so I'm inexperienced, but there is a barrier there."

"What do you do with virgins?" She knew little about the marital act because her mother had never discussed it with her.

"I would push through the barrier, but it will sting and you will likely bleed."

"But I had blood on my legs when they found me. Never mind. All the more reason for you to push through it. If I still have my maidenhead, I choose to gift it to you."

"Anna, if this is true and you are a virgin, then everything has been a lie. Everything! Why was our betrothal broken for a lie?"

She cupped his face and kissed him hard, a deep kiss that she hoped would make him forget about the rest of the world. Nothing could take this man away from her. Not a lie, not her sire, not even her king.

"I care only about us, David. Make love to me. Make me yours. 'Tis what we both want, is it not? You have not changed your mind, have you?" She gazed into his confused eyes, doing what she could to wipe away his doubt. Suddenly, it was as if a wave of water had washed over them from the heavens above, blessing them for being honest and true. She watched as the uncertainty faded from his gaze, replaced by a look of adoration that humbled her.

His words came out in a tone she'd grown to love. He was a man who knew his own mind, a man of strong character and moral values. A man she could always trust. "Nay,

I have not changed my mind. I love you and this is what was meant to be." David teased her a bit more, then took her lips in a searing kiss before he plunged into her. She squealed from the slight pain, but a sense of elation and empowerment followed it. No one had taken her virginity—she'd given it to the man she loved. David had smothered her scream fortunately. When he pulled back, his grin was the widest she'd ever seen.

"You're mine, Anna MacGruder. I handfast with you and promise to protect you, love you, and honor you for all my days. Do you accept me?"

Her heart about to burst with happiness, she whispered, "Aye."

Her insides still pinched, but she couldn't stop the smile on her own face from blossoming. "Oh, David, I'm so glad we did this. Forever. I'll love you forever, I promise."

He kissed her forehead and whispered, "Does it still hurt? I'll wait until your pain is gone."

"It only hurts a wee bit. 'Tis not so bad. Go ahead. What should I do?" She had no idea what happened next. The kitchen helpers had told her all about it, leaving out only that crucial part.

David reached down between them and touched her in a place between her legs that made her squirm. It was the lightest of touches, a caress that sent jolts of pleasure through her body.

"Does this feel good? I want you to find your pleasure with me."

"But I don't know how." She trusted him completely, so she said it without embarrassment. Rather than reply, he increased the pressure of his thumb. He dropped his head to her breast and used his tongue to caress her nipple in a way that made her want to shout with delight. Both of them began breathing faster.

David drove into her and pleasure rippled through her core, the sensations driving her to do things she never would have considered. She spread her legs wider, and he increased his pace, thrusting into her at a rate that consumed her entire being.

Her ability to think coherent thoughts left her. Her focus was solely on David and their bodies, how well they fit together, and how wonderful it felt to have him inside her. She closed her eyes, and he kissed her again, a slow, tantalizing kiss that made her moan, though she squelched the sound as best she could. She longed for something, but she didn't know what. She followed his lead, doing her best to keep up with his movements.

Her body thrummed with an urgency she couldn't control until something shattered deep within her, releasing a decadent pleasure that rushed through her. She dug her nails into his shoulders, trying to hang on to the exhilaration as long as she could.

David growled, his hands now cupping her bottom, tugging her as close as he could until he convulsed over her, his release shooting through him the same way hers had, or so she guessed by the way he shuddered, his eyes closed and his hands locked in a grip on her hips that she wished he'd never release. Small contractions continued to rock her insides as he finished, planting his seed deep inside her. The thought of a wee bairn blossomed in her mind as he sighed and nuzzled her neck.

"Did I please you, sweeting?"

"Aye, you could not tell? Did I please you?"

He smirked. "You could not tell by the sounds I made?"

"I think we were both pleased, but I hope no one else heard us."

"Are you sore? Will it bother you if I pull out? We shouldn't stay like this for long, just in case." The concern in her loved one's gaze almost brought her to tears. No one else would ever care about her the way this man did.

"You cannot hurt me. Do what you must. I'm just sad we can't enjoy each other in peace." She ran her hand down the side of his face, then rubbed the stubble on his jaw.

"Someday, you'll have no one to worry about but you and me in our verra own bed."

She could only dream of such happiness.

———◆———

DAVID KISSED HER LIPS AND moved to the side once he pulled out. "My love, I would like naught more than to sit by your side, but I think 'tis best if I take my leave. I'm going to make sure my cousins are here before I take you away with me. I promise to return momentarily." He stood and put his plaid on, pausing when he noticed the blood.

This was the evidence that Anna had truly been untouched. He finished arranging his plaid and sat on the side of the bed. "Anna, I have blood on me. Will you allow me to look at you?"

She nodded, chewing on her bottom lip as she lifted her chemise, allowing him to look before she peered over the edge of the gown.

He smiled at her. "You were a virgin, but no more. Now you belong to me."

"Oh, David. I'm so happy."

At that moment, the door flew open and the abbess stepped inside, two nuns behind her.

"What is going on in here? Why are you here?"

CHAPTER TWELVE

———◆———

THE ABBESS GASPED AND FELL backward when her eyes fell on Anna's thighs and the smears of blood between them. The two nuns behind her caught her and Anna dropped her gown, her cheeks flaming.

David was horrified at first—this was perhaps the least appropriate place for them to have made love for the first time—but his mood quickly turned to elation. This was exactly what they needed. He squeezed Anna's hand and said, "I know this will be unpleasant, but trust me."

He knew the way of the nobility, their king, and even his parents. This would work.

His voice was strong. "Sisters, I humbly apologize for the indelicacy of this situation, but I respectfully request that you bear witness to this event." He nodded to Anna, who cast her gaze downward as he lifted her chemise. "I have taken her maidenhead. Before this happened, we handfasted—I pledged my troth to her and she accepted. If you bring a monk or a priest, I would appreciate it, as I have the same evidence on me. I'll marry her as soon as you find a priest willing to marry us."

Anna nodded her agreement. "Aye, I wish to marry him right away."

Micheil's large body appeared in the doorway, his eyes wide. He must have heard David's request because his first words were, "I'll find a priest. Do not move any of you."

A short time later, two young priests came to the chamber. They took one look at the abbess, and one of them turned to the two nuns and said, "Get her to a chamber and find her something to drink before she faints. Her color is quite poor."

The three of them left quickly. The priest stared at David before he nodded at his plaid. "Lift it."

David did as he was asked, then dropped it as soon as he noted the recognition in the men's eyes.

The priest turned to Anna. "Were you a willing participant in this, or did he force himself on you?"

She stared at him, confusion written all over her face, but recognition finally dawned in her eyes. "Nay, he did not force himself on me. David would never do such a thing."

David's sire gave him a sharp look. "David, step outside so the priests can question Anna."

As soon as he left the room, Anna shouted, "Nay, he did not want to do it. I begged him. I wish to marry David Drummond. We handfasted first. He is my husband in my eyes."

David could hear her voice hitch. How he wished he could go to her...

His father moved toward him, no doubt to berate him, but instead he leaned over and whispered, "Well done, lad."

He had no idea how to answer that, so he simply nodded.

Then his father added, "However, I cannot help but wonder why Lorne MacGruder informed us that she'd lost her maidenhead."

What his sire said next nearly undid him. "Och, well, seems you've found it. Can't refute evidence like that. The king would never refuse you now. Smart, verra smart." He chuckled a slight bit. "Still, I'll be sure to ask Lorne Mac-Gruder about his lies."

Anna's mother came down the passageway and hurried toward the door. "Anna, what are you doing in the cellar? I fell asleep for but a moment, and you disappeared."

David took a step toward her. "My lady, I have renewed

my offer of marriage to your daughter, and she has accepted."

Her eyes widened and she pushed past him. She stood in the doorway of the room, frozen, her eyes taking in the situation. David swore he saw a wee smile cross her face before she regained control of her expression.

She marched in past the priests to join her daughter.

A few moments later, the priests emerged. "We will proceed with marriage. 'Tis nearly dawn. Be here at high sun on the morrow. We must advise the king and the lass's sire of what has transpired. We understand he was not supportive of this match, but we will insist upon it. Once the king is made aware, he will also support your claim. Saddens me to see it happen this way, but there is no doubt of your claim."

"Forgive me, Fathers, for my indiscretion. No disrespect of Anna or the abbess was intended." He could feel the blush rise on his cheeks. He wasn't quite sure how to apologize for something he didn't regret, though he understood the indelicacy of the situation. "May I talk to her again?"

Both priests shook their heads in unison. "Nay. Go home and return on the morrow."

"Will you promise me you will not allow her sire to take her from here? I need your pledge on this. He is against our marriage."

"But the king supported your betrothal. Of that we are certain. So we are only moving up a wedding that was blessed by our king."

"Aye, 'tis true, but her sire does not support our marriage, so my fear is he will do something sinister to remove her…"

The priest stopped him with a wave of his hand. "He will not remove her. I've seen what happened with my own eyes and I vow you will marry her, regardless of her sire's wishes. The king and our Lord both support your union under the circumstances. Be here on the morrow."

His sire clasped his shoulder and ushered him around. "I promise, Fathers, we will have him here promptly at midday."

They didn't speak on the way out. His father hurried him toward the door and said, "Where is your brother? He disappeared right after you did. I guessed you would leave, but I didn't expect Daniel to follow."

David stopped and turned to his sire. "'Tis time for us to stop treating him differently because of his injury. He made the comment that no one would notice his absence because none of us expect anything of him."

"Och, we proved him wrong, did we not? Your mother is frantic."

David rolled his eyes. His mother was known to be dramatic at times. "Don't you mean desperate?"

His father guffawed. 'Desperate' was his mother's favorite word to describe her mood when she was upset about something.

When his father's laughter died down, David said, "'Tis time to allow Daniel to be a warrior. Papa, he's almost as strong with his sword arm as I am. He can control his horse with just his knees. I say we let him travel with our guards. He need not be in the front, but he should start to learn."

His father nodded. "I'll talk with your mother. But first, where the hell is he?"

"Probably around back with Will and Maggie." He led his father back to the pre-arranged meeting place where he'd left his horse, pleased to see his brother and cousins waiting for him.

"Do we need to storm the abbey?" Will asked. "I don't know what you did, but you certainly have the nuns and the monks in turmoil."

David grinned, and his father set his hand on his shoulder. "Nay, all is well. David is to marry Anna on high sun on the morrow. Hope you'll all join us."

Micheil then addressed Daniel. "Part of me wishes to wring your neck for upsetting your mother, but I applaud you for following your brother. He's a wee bit headstrong and—" he nodded to Will and Maggie, "—I'm pleased he wasn't here on his own. We were all ordered to return to Drummond Castle, so that's where I'm going. If David wishes to tell you the details of all that transpired, I'll leave it up to him."

David gave them the briefest details, and he was quite certain his sire could hear the hoots and hollers of the other young people as they all made their way home.

THE DAY OF HIS WEDDING, David hopped out of bed and headed to the loch for a bath. Yesterday had been a very long day. They'd arrived home the eve before when it was nearly dusk, and they'd sat up with his mother explaining all to her.

Then she'd lit up inside, excited by the prospect of planning the wedding. His sire waved him away. "Allow her to do what she must. She'll get in touch with the family and send a messenger to the king. I'm sure he'll be expecting one once he receives the missive from the monks. You have not slept and are to go to bed. Your wedding is tomorrow."

Daniel had clapped him on the back, drawing their father's attention to him. "Daniel, you are going to bed, also. No more chasing until the morrow. The priests will take care of everything, and if they forget, your mother will see it done."

His father had actually pushed him and his brother toward the staircase.

"But I must speak to Sweeney," he'd objected, to which his sire had replied, "I'll speak with Sweeney. You and Daniel need to rest. Then I'm heading to my own bed."

"But where did Maggie and Will go? And the others?"

David asked.

Micheil snorted. "Don't you know that Uncle Logan raised his bairns to be just like him? They're all wanderers. Gavin couldn't sit still and neither could Maggie and Will. I think your uncle headed toward Edinburgh to see if he could learn aught there, and they followed him. Who knows where they are? I'm not worried. They'll be at your wedding."

His mother laughed. "Logan will get the news in the wind. I know not how he keeps up on all, but he does. They'll all be there, David, you can count on it."

He'd slept nearly the entire day away, and then he and his parents, his brother, and Sweeney had all rehashed their experiences and talked about the wedding.

Today was their day. Though they'd handfasted, today was the day he and Anna would stand in front of a priest to say their vows and declare their love for each other in front of everyone. He'd do everything he could to please his bride-to-be. He hoped his relatives would meet them at the abbey to celebrate the marriage, though Aunt Jennie and Uncle Aedan were not at home. He hadn't heard yet about Uncle Quade and Aunt Brenna. He loved the fact that the Grants and Ramsays were so close that he'd adopted most of the Grant family as aunts and uncles and cousins.

The sun shone brightly over the summer foliage as he trekked out to the loch. He didn't want company, he just wished to wallow in the water and the day, enjoy everything he could about his wedding day. While he still had concerns about Lorne MacGruder and whether or not he would accept the situation, he vowed he would not allow it to stop their marriage. Even if they were not officially married, he and Anna had handfasted, something that was an accepted—though not common—practice.

He still couldn't stop the wee niggling in his mind that something would go wrong, though his sire and mother had worked hard to convince him that with the king and the priests on his side, Lorne MacGruder would not get his way.

His mother was busy preparing his leine, the Drummond dress plaid, and everything else necessary for the wedding of the heir to the lairdship. Trusting that everything would take place as commanded by the priests, he dropped his plaid on the grass and dove in, relishing the cool water.

Lying on his back, he kicked around in the serene water, listening to the calls of the birds, which seemed as pleased about the day ahead as he was. He scrubbed himself, washed his hair, and swam a few laps before climbing out and walking over to his horse to dry. There he donned his clothing again.

Anna was to be his wife today.

The loch was an appropriate place for him to be because he thought this was the very spot where he'd decided to make her his wife. They'd come here on one of her flower-hunting expeditions, and she'd practically bubbled over with excitement when he'd climbed through nettles and thick bushes to gather a bunch of wildflowers for her. They'd been at the peak of a precarious hill, and he'd always had a slight fear of heights.

"David, it's so beautiful. Do you know if you dig plants up with the roots attached you can replant them somewhere else? When I marry, I will plant wildflowers and flowering bushes all across the front of my castle. And then I wish to plant a garden behind the castle with a bench to relax on and mayhap a fountain for the birds to splash around in. What do you think?" She'd glanced at him with such admiration that he knew in that moment he'd do anything it took to see that expression on her face again.

"I'm certain 'tis possible. Aunt Brenna has a garden much like the one you speak of, but she grows and harvests plants for healing. She tends it frequently, says it soothes her to have her hands in the dirt. You don't strike me as the kind of lass who would like to have your hands in the dirt." He brushed a smudge off her cheek, left by her thumb when she'd swept a bug away from her fine skin. Anna had the most beautiful complexion he'd ever seen. It often turned pink in the sun, giving her cheeks a rosy glow almost as fetching as her sweet lips. But what he loved most was the smattering of freckles that danced across her nose and took on a life of their own whenever she laughed. She wasn't overly fond of her freckles, but he adored them.

Someday he hoped he'd have a daughter with those same freckles.

She scowled, pushing her bottom lip out as she often did, and said, "Well, I could get the armorer to fashion me a small tool to dig with so my hands wouldn't be in the dirt all the time. Or use a shovel. Not that I would mind, but my mother would scold me if I came in covered with dirt."

David leaned over to kiss her cheek, making her giggle. "But when you are married, your mother may not live with you. You will be free to do as you choose." He kissed a path over to her lips and suckled the bottom one until she closed her eyes and sighed with pleasure.

When he finished torturing her, she whispered, "I fear I'm falling in love with you, David Drummond. You send chills up and down my spine whenever you are near. Is that not a true sign of love?"

He kissed her again, a tantalizing kiss meant to make her whimper in the way he loved. Her hands wrapped around his neck and tugged him closer.

She pulled back for just a moment and locked gazes with him. "Do you love me?"

What else could he call it? "Aye, I fear I lose my head whenever I'm around you. Someday, mayhap you'll be planting the garden behind our castle."

"Oh, David!" She jumped into his arms, wrapping her legs around his waist in a most unfeminine position. Pressed against her womanly parts, his cock hardened in an instant.

"Someday, I promise." And he'd meant it. David Drummond was a man of his word.

Aye, he'd decided that day that life with Anna MacGruder would be as sweet as the aroma of those wildflowers.

He headed back to the keep, pleased to see his mother at the hearth already, fussing with the Drummond crest. "My, but you are up early."

"Of course, 'tis my wedding day." He kissed her cheek and took a seat next to her.

She called to one of the servants arranging dishes on a nearby trestle table. "Would you bring David some porridge, please?"

"Aye, my lady," she said, walking over to the hearth. "Will there be aught else for you?"

"How are the meat pies coming along? The family will come back here to celebrate this eve. Stew and meat pies for all, whatever we have. Avelina said she'd try to make it here by this eve if they could, plus she said she'd send extra loaves of bread to feed all the lads."

"All is going as planned."

"I'll check on everything while you serve David. I'll return quickly." His mother gave him a reassuring smile and headed toward the kitchens.

Just then the door to the great hall burst open, and Filib MacGruder stood in the opening, panting.

"Filib? What is it?" David asked, but he already had a sinking feeling in his gut. It had been too easy.

"My sister is gone. My sire and mother went to see her this morn and she's gone. Is she here?"

"Hellfire, nay. She's not here, Filib." David thought he would lose all control. A cold sweat broke out on his face and his hands fisted at his side. He did not for one moment believe Filib's story. That bastard Lorne had stolen his wife again.

"Mama? I'm going to the abbey to kill the MacGruder!"

CHAPTER THIRTEEN

ANNA AWAKENED IN A DARK chamber. She attempted to sit, but her head hurt so badly, she moaned and fell back on the rough pallet.

This was not her normal bed. Nor was it the bed she'd been given in the abbey. Opening her eyes, she peered around the chamber in fear. Wherever she was, she wasn't alone—there were two other pallets, and she could hear soft snoring and quiet crying.

The place was damp and rank with the odor of body fluids. She had on a coarse wool gown that did not belong to her, and she felt as if she hadn't eaten in days. Forcing herself to sit up, she pushed against the thin pallet and set her feet on the floor at the side of the small bed.

The crying stopped instantly. Anna was finally able to discern another body on a pallet directly opposite her, a shadow of a figure that looked to be another lass close to her in age. A stranger.

"Where am I?" she whispered, afraid to speak too loudly. A door to her right led to a passageway lit by a torch large enough to shed light into the room now that her eyes had adjusted. The door was closed but had a small window at the top. Was she a prisoner again?

"In a deserted castle, part of the Channel of Dubh."

"The what?"

"Channel of Dubh. The dark channel is what they call it. 'Tis a network centered in Edinburgh and Ayr. They depend on ships for the transportation of merchandise, you see, so they need to be close to the firths."

"What merchandise?" Anna dreaded to hear the answer to her question. She folded her hands in her lap and gripped them together. If she were able to see them, she was certain there would be little color to them.

"Us." The lass sat up. "We're the merchandise. They sell us as though we're no better than a ball of wool. What's your name?"

"Anna," she said in a shaky voice. "And yours?"

"Mariana." She swiped the tears from her face in a gesture that told Anna exactly how frustrated she felt.

"How long have I been here?" Her brain seemed foggy again, much like it had been ever since the day she'd awakened in the forest.

"Someone brought you here yesterday. You've been sleeping ever since. I think you were given a potion. The man tried to wake you, but he couldn't."

At least a day had passed since she'd been with David, which meant today was likely supposed to be her wedding day. She forced herself to forget about the lost time and focus on what was happening to her. "I don't understand, Mariana. What are you talking about? What is this Channel of Dubh?" She had a sinking suspicion she knew exactly what Mariana was talking about. Hadn't David told her something about his Band of Cousins uncovering a group selling children? But they had killed the person responsible, if she recalled correctly. And yet...

If her head would clear of all of those blasted potions, surely she would remember.

"It's a network of bad men, I guess you could say. Men who try to operate outside the law without getting caught. They steal lasses and young lads, or pay coin for them, and sell them to the wealthy. Sometimes here in Scotland, other times in noble homes in England, others go across the sea to the East."

"How do you know all this, Mariana?" She could feel tears well in her eyes as the hopelessness of her situation dawned on her. She and David had finally pledged their troths to each other, and now she was here.

"Because my sire always threatened to send me and my sister here. He finally did it. 'Tis my sister sleeping on the other pallet." She pointed to the third pallet with a sadness that broke Anna's heart. She'd always wished for a sister.

"My sister is younger than I am, and she's unable to cope with the fact we've been given away. Our Mama died a few months ago, and my father said he can no longer take care of us. We did everything for him, cooking, cleaning, and all the needlework, but he wished to remarry and the woman he chose didn't want any bairns around."

"You lost your mother, too?" Life could be so cruel. How sad to lose one parent and then have the other sell you— a betrayal of the cruelest sort.

She knew exactly what that felt like. "How old are you?"

"I'm ten and eight, my sister Crisly is ten and three. Our mother was English, our sire is Scottish. She misses our mama so much that she's stopped caring what will happen to her. She stopped talking and only stares into space. I have to lead her around. The man yells at me, tells me that he won't be able to sell her if I don't get her talking. I hope he can't, so I don't push her too hard. She's too young to be raped. I'm old enough to understand what's coming for us."

The more Mariana talked, the more familiar it sounded. Memories continued to wash over her. David had told her all about his adventure in Edinburgh with his Band of Cousins.

"What's wrong?" Mariana asked.

"My betrothed," she said, rubbing her forehead. "David returned from a trip to Edinburgh not long ago. He and his cousins caught a man who was selling young bairns and trying to put them on a ship in the firth near Edinburgh. The lassies were quite a bit younger. They would have gone east…"

Her memory continued to fill in the missing bits and pieces.

Mariana reached over to grasp Anna's hand, squeezing it tight. "Did they get away?"

"Aye, they saved the lassies, though one was nearly dead when they found her in Edinburgh. I think David's cousin Maggie and her husband killed the man who was selling the bairns." A big grin crossed Anna's face as she recalled something else. "I remember David telling me how Maggie had punched and kneed a man between the legs. It allowed her to keep him down because it weakens men. David spent a few hours teaching me how to use a dagger, how to hold it, and where the best place was to stab a man." She paused, then asked, "Do you know where they're taking us?"

"I hear we are headed to Ayr," Mariana said. "We had to wait for someone to arrive, so I guess that was you. We may leave on the morrow or the next day."

Anna decided she was not giving up. Not now that she was this close to getting what she wanted. What she needed. Not when there were other lasses in the same horrible position as her. "We're getting away. Will you help me?"

"Of course, but there's only one problem." She glanced away as if she were shamed by her words.

Anna could see the tears mist her eyes again.

"If Crisly and I get out, where will we go? Papa does not want us. We have no home to return to."

A heat of anger rushed through Anna at the thought of what this fool had done to his own daughters. "You may come along with me. My father must have sold me, too. I don't know why, but he did not want to marry me to my betrothed. We will find my love, and he'll help us all."

"Who is your betrothed?"

"David Drummond."

Mariana gasped. "The handsome lad whose mother is laird of the Drummonds?"

"Ahhh, so you've heard of him?"

Mariana's eyes sparked with excitement. "Mama used to talk of his mother, how elegant and refined she is, and so beautiful. She thought the Drummonds were the nicest clan of all. You are verra fortunate. Well, you *were* verra fortunate. Why doesn't your papa want you to marry him? Is he nasty?"

"My David? Nay, he is wonderful. I have no idea. The betrothal has been set for a month, but I was abducted and left in the middle of the forest. My sire claimed I was raped so I couldn't marry David. He said nobles do not marry tainted lasses. But he lied. I don't understand. I always thought Papa loved me, but apparently he does not." She couldn't stop the tears from spilling onto her cheeks. Her life had been one travesty after another over the course of the last sennight.

She would not allow this to happen. She and David had handfasted, expressing their love for each other. Their time together had been magical.

"I'm not giving up. *We're* not giving up," she whispered, narrowing her gaze at the door to their prison. "I'll do what I must to get us away. I've had enough of men controlling our lives and telling us what to do. We're all going to be set free, you and me and Crisly." She'd made her mind up, and she would not give in to this farce, this mockery of justice, this Channel of Dubh. "When I get the chance, I will fight."

"And you'll truly find a place to live where Crisly could be happy? Could I stay with her?"

"Aye, there will be room for you at Drummond Castle. David's mother is wonderful, just like your mama told you."

"I have one question," Mariana said. "Where did those girls go when they were freed? Were they given to a nice family or sent to work for the nobility?"

"They were adopted into David's extended family. We can do this. If David's cousin Maggie can find the strength to defeat those horrible men, then so can we. Will you help me?"

A voice from the next pallet reached her ears. Crisly sat up and whispered, "I'll help you."

Mariana jumped up and moved next to her sister and hugged her. "I'm so glad you're back, Crisly. Now we have hope." She pointed her finger straight at Anna. "There's our hope right in front of us."

Anna sat up and squared her shoulders. "If Maggie Ramsay can do this, so can we. We're not getting on any ship. We'll find our way back to Crieff. David will be looking for me, and I plan to meet him halfway."

After their one night together, Anna MacGruder was not giving up on her husband.

She was stronger and more determined than ever.

CHAPTER FOURTEEN

———◆———

DAVID COULD SWEAR THE JOURNEY he made to Lochluin Abbey was the longest ride he'd ever taken. He'd finally thought everything was settled, that he'd out-smarted Anna's sire, but he'd made a crucial error.

Bastard. Rat bastard, as his cousin Loki would say.

How could the bastard have stolen his daughter from the abbey without anyone noticing? Why hadn't he been stopped? The man clearly thought he was invincible, but David intended to show him how very wrong he was.

To his surprise, there was a large collection of people gathered outside of the abbey, all of them yelling. He was even more surprised when he saw King Alexander and his men had arrived. There stood the royal king in the middle of the mayhem listening to several people shouting. He could only guess that the king had received so many mis-sives from the MacGruders and the Drummonds that he'd set out to settle the issue himself.

The abbess had her arms crossed defensively in front of her, and the monks and priests on either side of her had such red faces they looked on the verge of dropping into a dead faint. The MacGruders stood opposite them in a clear challenge.

David dismounted and moved over to the group, waving his arms. He wished to be a part of this discussion since it was his betrothed they were discussing. No one addressed him until Lorne MacGruder set eyes upon him, and his reaction was immediate and unprovoked. He shoved his way out of the crowd and headed straight for David.

He hit him square in the chest with the palm of his hand, much to David's surprise. He stumbled backward but caught himself before he fell to the ground.

"Where is she? I know 'twas you," he bellowed. "You've kidnapped my daughter from me. I want her back. Where is she? Confess, or I'll have you hung."

Filib grabbed his sire on either side and yanked him backward. David couldn't have been more stunned. If Lorne was responsible for Anna's abduction, the man was one hell of an actor.

David knew how to act in front of his king. He ignored MacGruder, moving around him to greet King Alexander.

"Good day to you, my king." He bowed and then took a step closer. "I'm pleased you have arrived."

As he spoke, he caught sight of two riders approaching. Out of the corner of his eye, he recognized Maggie and Will. Pleased he had more allies here, he returned his focus to the king.

"Greetings to you, David of Drummond. How does your dear mother fare?"

"She is well, I expect her to be here in a short time. May I inquire about my betrothed? She was here when I left the night before last, but word has reached me that she is missing. Where could she have gone?"

"Ah, so you have heard about our dilemma. I've been doing my best to uncover the truth of the matter, but no one seems to know anything beyond that your betrothed was last seen when she broke her fast yesterday. I don't know if she left on her own or if she had assistance in this disappearance. What say you?"

David replied, "I know naught about this. I was on Drummond land preparing for our wedding. If I had wished to kidnap her, I would have done so the other night. I was hoping to be a married man by this evening." His voice cracked a little as he said it. Was Anna hale? Would he find her? The pressure of not knowing bore down on him. "Have you any suspects at all? If not, I certainly do."

"And who would be your primary suspect, lad?" his king asked, crossing his arms in front of him, his gaze boring into David's.

"Her sire, of course. He has done his best to put our marriage asunder. Ever since the unexplained attack on Anna, which she barely remembered at all, he has done his best to keep us apart, even attempting to betroth her to another when you had already blessed our union. He attempted to marry her to Gilroy Walters just recently, without your approval, my king."

"Is this true, Lorne? I heard of this attempt to undermine my orders, but I'd like the full story from you." He lifted his chin toward the MacGruder, whose face was now as red as the first cherries in summer.

Lorne MacGruder paused, taking his glare from David back to King Alexander. "We were awaiting your approval. I sent you a missive about the attack. I was doing my best to salvage her reputation, my king. This had naught to do with a lack of respect for you. I did it out of respect for my daughter. She was devastated when she discovered she was no longer untouched, too embarrassed to marry the heir to Drummond Castle."

"That's a lie and you know it, MacGruder!" He'd had enough of Lorne MacGruder. "Where is she? Who did you pay to take her away? Is she with Walters?" He grabbed the front of the man's tunic and lifted him a few feet off the ground, turning the bastard's face a strange shade of purple.

"Set him down, Drummond," the king said firmly. "You remind me of your uncle Logan. Where is he? I could use him about now."

Maggie, who'd approached them without speaking, spoke up. "He's on his way, my king."

David finally set MacGruder down. As soon as he did,

Lorne took a swing at him. "You took her. I heard you stole her maidenhead the other eve. My wife told me everything. You must have taken her and hidden her away."

His voice cracked in a most unusual way. David quirked a brow at him because he could swear he noticed a misting in the man's eyes. "Aye, what your wife said is true. No one was more surprised than me. Anna and I handfasted the eve before last. We pledged our troth to each other. I claimed her as my wife, but I honored the wishes of the abbess and the priests, who instructed me to return this morn to marry her at high noon in a religious ceremony. Whoever told you she lost her maidenhead in the previous attack lied."

MacGruder's face fell, a strange expression of failure crossing his features. Staring at the ground, he whispered, "Aye, 'twas my fault before. I paid someone to take her, leave her in the woods to be found. She was being watched so she couldn't be hurt."

"Why would you do such a thing, Lorne? She's your own flesh and blood," the king asked in evident shock.

"I did not want her married to David Drummond. There was no attack that night. She was just given something so she wouldn't remember aught. But I swear to you, I know not where she is now. I did not take her from here. I would have argued with you all morn about this marriage, but 'twas not me."

The words almost toppled David. This entire event had been because MacGruder did not want him to marry Anna? Why in the world had he accepted when David had offered for her? What had he and his parents done to earn such ill will from the man? But he had little time to think on it. If MacGruder was telling the truth, then who did take Anna? He needed to focus on the love of his life and find her before it was too late.

King Alexander said, "I'm going inside to speak with the abbess and the priests. I'll let you know if I discover aught

of value. And I go alone." He gave a pointed look to both
David and Lorne MacGruder. "You two are to stay outside,
on opposite sides of the courtyard."

David nodded, spun on his heel and tipped his head to
Maggie and Will, who now stood behind him, indicating he wished to talk with them in private. They found a
bench in a secluded area not far from the abbey, though
none of them sat down.

Four words from Maggie got their conversation headed
in the right direction.

"Do you believe him?"

David sighed, staring into the gray clouds over their
heads. "I really don't want to. I want to believe he did it, but
I was close enough to see the tears in his eyes. MacGruder
hasn't shed many tears in his lifetime. I don't believe he did
it as a ruse."

"And he admitted to setting up the ploy over her maidenhead to get her away from you. Why would he admit to
something so damning but not speak to his involvement in
this escapade?" Will asked.

Maggie said, "Oh, 'tis possible for certes. He's told so
many lies that he may no longer recognize the truth. The
question I have is why is he so dead set against his daughter
marrying a Drummond, let alone the future laird of the
clan? It makes no sense to me."

"I cannot answer that. He's always seemed reluctant
about the match, but his objections were never so serious
as this." David ran his fingers through his hair as he started
his pacing again. He had to do something, go after her,
search the area.

He couldn't just sit here and wait, feeling helpless.

"Is there anyone else you suspect could be involved in
this?" Will asked.

David shrugged his one shoulder. "Other than Gilroy
Walters, the man her sire promised her to?"

"What has he to gain from this marriage?"

David snorted. "Someone young and beautiful to warm his bed and take care of his four bairns."

"Mayhap there's been some coin involved somewhere," Maggie added.

David replied, "Nay, I think not. Neither is wealthy. Mac-Gruder could gain much more from our alliance."

Will stroked his beard. "Is there bad blood between your clans?"

"Nay! Not until this incident. At least, not to my knowledge. But the way he says my name makes me believe there *was* bad blood." David paced in a small area for a few moments and stopped. "I'd like to make a request."

Maggie said, "We'll do whatever you'd like. Just tell us."

"I'd appreciate the support of the full Band of Cousins. Can we call a meeting and make plans? I have to find her, but Scotland is too large an area for me to cover on my own."

To his surprise, a voice called to him from afar. "I'm glad to help."

He turned to see Daniel headed their way, Sweeney directly behind him. David couldn't keep the smile from his face. "Your assistance would be most welcome." He clasped his brother's shoulder as he joined the three of them, nodding to his friend Sweeney.

"Good," Daniel said. "Because I'm not leaving. I learned to get past my injury long ago. Now 'tis time for everyone else to catch up with me."

Sweeney patted him on the back, then turned to face David. "Why must you insist on traveling alone all the time? You know the heir to a lairdship shouldn't run off on his own. Take both of us along on all your jaunts so your mother doesn't cut my bollocks off, would you? She's daft when you're missing."

"What do you say, Maggie," Daniel asked, his eyes hopeful, "may I join the cousins?"

"So long as you agree that everything we do is confidential. You cannot discuss it with the other Drummond guards or your friends. And Sweeney, I expect the same from you. Keep up with my cousins, would you?"

"Accepted. What's the plan?"

David said, "We'll put one together while we wait for the others to arrive. We must first send missives."

"Nay. Already done, cousin. Gavin and Gregor will be here soon. The Grants should be here by nightfall. We'll have everything ready by the time they arrive."

"Do you have a lead?" David asked in surprise.

"Aye," Will replied. "MacGruder admitted he paid for someone to steal Anna away. We'll talk to King Alexander first, ask him to have MacGruder tell all, but mayhap he used the exact same channel we've heard whisperings about of late."

David sucked in his breath. Though it was terrible to think of Anna in such a situation, he felt a slight stirring of hope inside. He'd be willing to go from firth to firth to find his sweet Anna, but if they had a lead…"Channel? What channel?"

"The Channel of Dubh."

Hellfire. David kneaded his forehead. Whatever it was, it couldn't be good.

Who would name their operation the channel of darkness?

CHAPTER FIFTEEN

A NNA HAD REVIEWED THEIR PLAN with Mariana
and Crisly. The younger girl was to remain completely
mute in a bid to convince their captor she still could not
talk at all. They would count on her to steal a dagger for
Anna to use. Crisly remembered seeing three daggers in
the chamber above. Since Anna was the only one who'd
had much experience with a dagger, it would fall on her to
actually fight their captor. Mariana had only seen one man,
and if he truly were here without any others, she thought
she could manage to do enough damage to allow them
to get away. She hoped they would be allowed out of this
filthy chamber soon. The stench was nauseating, and they
desperately needed fresh air.

"How did you become so strong, Anna?" Mariana whispered. "My sire never taught us how to use a dagger."

"'Tis as I said. David taught me, but I also practiced a bit
on my own when I was younger."

"Truly? My sire would have thrashed me for touching a
dagger," Mariana whispered.

The words immediately summoned a memory, so strong
it practically sent her reeling. Anna had almost forgotten
all about it. In fact, she hadn't even mentioned it to David.

As a lassie, she'd been so jealous of her much older brothers that she would try to do aught she could to be just like
them. Filib had understood, and he'd instructed her on
the use of a wooden sword. She'd practiced and practiced

with it, believing that someday she could be just like the warriors who defended their castle.

Of course, Ossian had called her a foolish chit for thinking a lass could learn to fight. He'd never been kind to her, though he'd certainly gotten worse over the years.

Then that fateful day had come along. She'd found a real dagger on the ground and picked it up, going after Ossian in play.

She'd been no more than five summers, too young to understand the difference between real and play until she swung the knife at her elder brother from behind and it embedded in the back of his leg. Ossian had screamed, reaching behind him as the blood began to flow down his leg, and her sire had come running.

Her father had pulled the knife out of Ossian's leg and bellowed, "Who did this to you?"

"Anna did it, Papa. Anna!"

She'd been so frightened, she'd just stared at her sire in shock, unable to understand what she'd done. She'd swung her much bigger wooden sword at Filib many times without hurting him at all. Why had this smaller one injured Ossian so?

"I'm sorry, Ossian."

Her father had picked up her up, thrown her over his knee, and proceeded to give her a thrashing she'd never forget. He kept yelling at her. "He's my heir. How dare you hurt my heir!"

She'd heard that declaration over and over again as he continued to spank her bottom, sending wave after wave of pain through her. He'd never hit her before that moment. Her mother had come running out of the keep, and when her father finally finished punishing her, he scooped her under his arm and tossed her to her mother. "She doesn't belong out here with the lads. Do your job, woman."

That was the last time she'd been allowed to run with the boys outside. Her mother had made certain she didn't step out with the lads again. Her place was inside the keep, she was told, learning how to use a needle and be a lady.

After her punishment, her bottom was so sore she couldn't sit down for days, instead standing near the hearth and cuddling her fabric doll, wondering why her sire had hurt her so. His ire had hurt her almost as much as the thrashing.

Fortunately, his anger had quickly softened. He'd come in one day, set a pillow on his lap and pulled her up onto it. "Anna, lassie, I'm sorry I lost my temper with you. You deserved the thrashing, but mayhap 'twas a bit too harsh for one so young and delicate. You must not hurt your brother. He's the heir to the MacGruder land. He'll be laird someday. He could have died from the fever."

"But I could be laird if he died, or Filib. You're our papa, too."

"You're a lassie, sweet, and lassies are not lairds. And Filib? Well, he's Filib. He could never be given the lairdship. Nay, Ossian will be laird when I'm gone."

After that, she hadn't questioned that sons were more important than daughters. As her mother had told her more than once, it was the way of the world.

"Anna?" Mariana rubbed her arm, wresting her out of the memory.

Instinctively, her hand moved to her bottom and rubbed it, as if the pain her sire had caused her so long ago were still there.

It was, only it had moved to a different place, deep inside her heart. Lately, the man she'd loved and respected for her whole life had turned into someone she didn't recognize or understand. She wished she knew why.

"I'm sorry, Mariana. Your words brought an old memory to the surface. A thrashing my papa gave me for an accident with a dagger."

Crisly reached out and squeezed her hand, silently offering her support.

"Hopefully, we'll get our chance soon, and we'll run far, far away." What she didn't say was that she wished they could find a place to live where women were valued instead of being sold or traded, where men weren't threatened by a woman who could think. A place where women weren't told to stay inside the keep because that was where they belonged. Surely Drummond Castle, where a woman was the laird, was such a place. David had also told her about his aunt Gwyneth, who'd won the reputation of being the best archer in all of Scotland. He said he'd watched her compete, and no man could beat her, though many had tried.

She was tired of being judged just because she was a lass. There were no lads being sold with her. What was wrong with men?

She sat back down on the pallet, reviewing all the different ways she could hurt a man, when the sound of footsteps carried down the passageway.

She stood up and turned to the doorway, deciding she would rather face her enemy head on. A young lad opened the door and nodded to them. "Follow me."

Anxious to escape the stench of the chamber, she glanced over her shoulder to make sure Mariana and Crisly were behind her, then followed the lad down the passageway and up a staircase into a single chamber with a door to the outside. Before now, she'd never seen a building this small with a cellar. She blinked at the pain of the sudden exposure to light after many hours of darkness. A single man stood in the doorway with his back to them. Something was familiar about him, though she couldn't quite say what. He gave instructions over his shoulder. "Tie up the older two. Leave the dumb one alone. She'll not run off on you. I'll probably have to toss her off the cart on the side of the road, for I've no doubt no one will buy her."

"Who are you?" Anna asked the man in the doorway, unable to help herself. The lad grabbed her hands together behind her back and tied the rope tight while she spoke.

"You dare to speak to me? Shut your mouth, whore." He spun around to glare at her.

As soon as she laid eyes on him, she gasped.

"Och, you do remember me, *my lady* MacGruder?"

He spoke her name with a teasing lilt, one she hated.

"You'll not be a lady much longer, will you? My apologies for the part I played in your downfall."

The man with the scarred face stepped forward until he was a hand's length away from her. "On second thought, I have no apologies. I was paid quite well to give you a potion to make you sleep and then smear chicken blood on your thighs. I made more coin for your little job than I usually do. And now I'm about to make a bundle on you."

He brought his finger up and ran it down her cheek.

She jerked her face away from him and he chuckled.

"You are a pretty one. I'd take you myself, but you're far more valuable as a virgin. 'Tis not often I make double for one lass."

"I hope the sheriff catches you." She needed to distract him from the discussion of her virginity, afraid her blush would alert him to the change in her. This entire experience had altered her. It was more than what had happened with David at the abbey. She was more confident, more certain of her ability to change her destiny, yet she wished to hide that confidence from him. It was in her best interest to appear meek.

He laughed. "All it takes is a few coins to shut the sheriff up."

"Who paid you? At least tell me that much."

The scarred man shrugged. "I've sworn no secrecy. Your father hired me to make it look as though you were raped, and he hoped to cast suspicion on your lover. Drummond, is that his name? Quite an easy job. And now that you're ruined, I can sell you to the highest bidder. A noble lass with her maidenhead intact will get me a nice pile of coin, especially one as beautiful as you. The greenish eyes, the red hair…do you know how much men in the East will pay for that coloring? Their women are all dark-haired. They'll pay just to see if the curls between your legs match your hair color, and if they do, I can get even more. I already checked you." He guffawed as soon as he saw her blush.

Anna wished to cover her ears and hear no more. She wished to yell to the heavens that she was no longer a virgin, but then she feared he'd insist on checking for himself. Or perhaps it would give him the freedom he wished to abuse her himself. The state of her maidenhead was none of his business.

His words sunk deep into her belly, like a stone that would carry her far below the water in the loch, down into the deepest, darkest place. Her own sire had sold her. Why? What had she done to deserve it?

Mariana whispered. "Do not fret, Anna. My sire sold us, also."

She understood Mariana's words were meant to console her, but instead they lit a fire inside her. Men sold their own daughters.

Scarface, her new name for him, said, "Och, but I see the disappointment in your eyes. However, 'twas not your sire who gave you up this time. Someone else sold you to me, and only under the condition that I sell you across the water."

She frowned, wondering what he could be talking about.

"Och, you understand. 'Tis someone who hates you. I've never met this man before, and I don't know his name, nor do I care what 'tis. I gave him coin this time, though I'll get much more for you on the shore of the firth."

Her eyes widened, wondering what he could be talking about.

"Aye, 'tis true." He grinned from ear to ear, stretching the scar until it turned a strange shade of pink. "You're bound for a large cargo ship awaiting us in the firth. You'll never see Scotland again."

Stars above, what had they done? They were already tied up and soon they'd be headed for the firth. Sweat broke out across her brow. They were about to be put on a ship.

And she had no dagger in her hand to stop it.

CHAPTER SIXTEEN

———◆———

D AVID HEARD THE APPROACH OF horses and was pleased to see the new arrivals. Will and Maggie turned to see who they were while Daniel did his usual and wandered. Though they were still a distance away from the abbey, he could recognize his parents and their accompaniment of Drummond guards. Since Gavin, Gregor, and Uncle Logan had spent the night on Drummond land, they rode with his parents.

He greeted his cousins and uncle first, then waited for his parents before he filled everyone in on the situation. Once he explained the situation, he turned to Gavin and Gregor. "Tell us all again what you found at Walters's keep? Was he in residence?" He'd already spoken to them last eve, but he wanted to make sure everyone knew what had transpired.

"Aye," Gavin said. "I doubt he moved at all. I crept in the back and saw him pouting in his hall. He doesn't have a large force of guards.

Gregor added, "But he has some wild bairns who ran the entire hall unfettered."

"Who's in charge?" Uncle Logan asked. "Are those not the royal mounts I saw near the stables?"

"Aye," Maggie said. "King Alexander is inside."

Diana and Micheil joined them, and after another round of greetings, David's mother turned to him and pointedly asked, "Any idea where she is?"

"Nay," David said. "Lorne admitted to being the one who had her stolen away before, but he claims he had naught to do with this. No one saw anyone leave. The last time she was seen was yesterday morn. She's disappeared."

"And what does the king say?"

"He is speaking with the abbess and the monks," Will said. "We'll speak with him before we make our next move. See if he's uncovered aught and advise him of our plan."

"Your plan?" Logan asked.

David nodded. "Maggie and Will have been looking into an underground channel that funnels lassies to the firths to be sold. That says Edinburgh or Ayr to me, so I think that's where we head first."

"Maggie, have you any new information about this network?" Micheil asked.

"Only that it operates at night, which is why it's called 'Dubh,' and no one talks about it. I don't know who runs the operation, but it's a big secret we haven't been able to uncover yet. We'll keep trying."

"Hopefully, we'll learn something new," Will agreed.

David said to the group, "I've asked my cousins to help me search all of Scotland if need be. The Grants are on their way, so we'll split up. Sweeney, Daniel, and I will go in one direction, mayhap to Ayr; the Grants can go to Glasgow; and Maggie, Will, Gavin, and Gregor can search Edinburgh."

Logan nodded. "Your sire and I will stay here to await the Grants. When they arrive, we'll send them along their way. I do ask that you do as Will suggested and wait until the king apprises us of what he's learned. 'Tis not unusual for the monks to keep something quiet."

They stood there in uncomfortable silence, David pacing back and forth. The door opened and a monk addressed them. "The king would like to speak to you in our gathering hall. The MacGruders also wish to speak with you."

The group made their way inside. David hoped the king

had uncovered useful information. His parents and aunt and uncle greeted the king and thanked him for personally intervening in the matter. King Alexander was apparently in a hurry because he motioned for everyone to take a seat at the chairs situated around the large hall. There were several tables arranged on opposite sides of the room. The walls were stark, covered with religious symbols of various types—crosses mostly. A small hearth sat on the outside wall while the tables ran parallel to each other.

Once the Drummonds and Ramsays sat down, the door opened and the MacGruders entered, taking three seats on the other side of the aisle.

Where was Ossian?

Lorne held onto Jean tightly, even after they'd taken their seats, for she looked as though she were about to faint. Filib sat on the other side of her.

King Alexander addressed the group, saying the same as what he'd said earlier in the day. He added that the monks and the abbess had no further information to give them.

Once he finished, David's sire asked the question that had been on David's lips, "Where is Ossian?"

His comment shifted everyone's attention to the Mac-Gruders. David heard a gasp from his mother seated next to him. He turned to her and whispered, "Mama? What is it?"

"Naught," she replied. "I've been trying to understand why someone looks familiar, and I think I've figured it out." She patted David's hand. "Naught to concern yourself about just now."

Her condition improved, and David glanced at his sire, who appeared equally confused, before returning his attention to their king.

Lorne MacGruder spoke up and said, "My apologies for what I did before. I had my own reasons to prevent my daughter from marrying David, so I attempted a foolish hoax. My daughter was not attacked, as you now know, and it was wrong of me, but I had naught to do with her disappearance yesterday. I beg you to find my daughter. She is innocent in all of this. I've sent Ossian out to search for her with our guards. I have no idea what's become of her." MacGruder's face was weathered, almost defeated. He'd engineered a fiasco, and now it had turned on him.

With King Alexander here as witness to all that was going on, David didn't doubt the man was concerned. David glanced at Will, wondering what he thought of the man's speech. Did he believe him? Will pursed his lips, apparently still unsure.

"Does anyone have any suggestions?" the king asked. "If not, we'll organize search parties. I can call on the Cameron guards to assist the Drummond and MacGruder guards. Is there aught else anyone has to say?"

All was quiet, and the king was about to speak again when a small figure opposite David stood up, clearing her throat. "I have something I need to say."

Jean MacGruder glanced at her husband and son before stepping away from them.

"Jean, you will keep your mouth closed about this issue," Lorne said, his face instantly going red again. "This is private family issue."

"Nay, Lorne. It is not. Not any longer. These lies have hurt too many, and it stops now."

She had the attention of everyone in the room.

"Jean," Lorne shouted. "Sit down and be quiet, or I'll…"

King Alexander said, "Allow her to speak, MacGruder, or I'll send *you* out of the building."

MacGruder bit his lip, but his fury was visible to all. He was so upset that he leapt up from his chair and began pacing back and forth, his head shaking.

Before Jean could speak, Diana stood, gripping the table in front of her. She lifted her finger and pointed to Filib.

"I've been trying to understand why Filib appears familiar to me, but now I know. His eyes, his smile…oh, Papa."

Jean nodded to her and grabbed her son's hand, who had the same surprised expression on his face as David's mother.

"Forgive me, Lord, in this house of yours." Jean bowed her head as tears flowed down her cheeks. Then she lifted her head and stared directly at Diana.

"Meet your brother, Filib."

———————

ANNA WAS FRANTIC. SHE AND the other lasses had been placed in a large cart covered in blankets to hide their bindings in case they passed anyone along the way, but they never did. There had not yet been an opportunity for them to escape, and Scarface was urging the horses along at such a punishing speed, Anna feared such an opportunity would not present itself. They barreled ever closer to the Firth of Clyde and the impending cargo ship that would be their home for the next few weeks or months or however long it would take them to arrive at their destination in the East.

Scarface hadn't pushed Crisly out of the cart yet, though the farther they traveled and the more the horse foamed at the mouth, the greater her fear grew that he would hurt Crisly before they were in a position to do anything about it. When she thought she was about to spill the contents of her bladder all over the cart, he suddenly stopped and yelled to his young partner, "I've got to pish. Allow them to go one at a time, just keep them tied up."

Finally, they would get a chance to do something. Eager to relieve herself as quickly as possible so she wouldn't miss the opportunity to act, Anna rushed off to the side and squatted behind a bush. She heard Scarface yell, "Let her go. She can't hear you, dumb arse."

Moments later, Crisly showed up in front of her with a smile on her face and a small knife in her hands. Relief radiated through Anna as she held out her hands and the young girl cut the bindings. Anna took the knife, then tucked it in inside the sleeve of her gown, holding her hands together at the small of her back as if they were still tied there.

While Mariana moved behind the bushes, Scarface came out from behind a tree and said to Anna, "Get back in the cart. We're moving on at once."

She jutted her chin up. "I need help. I cannot get in with my hands tied behind my back."

Scarface shook his head. "Why must you women be so helpless? Just jump and fall in."

She shook her head silently.

"So be it." He lumbered toward her and dropped his hands low to scoop her into his arms and toss her in. She swung her hand out and buried the knife deep in his neck.

Scarface gagged and fell back, his hand going to the blood now spurting out from his neck, shock painted across his face as he looked at her. He crumpled to the ground, the life force leaking out of him. His partner came out from behind the trees at the same time as Mariana emerged from the bushes. Anna ran over and kicked him in the groin at once. He hadn't seen her coming because he couldn't take his eyes off his bleeding friend.

He groaned and fell to the ground after he turned away from her.

"Quick, Mariana!" Anna said. "Get on his horse and I'll cut this one free from the cart. I'll put Crisly on behind you."

They made quick with their plan, freeing the horses while the lad still lay writhing on the ground. Mariana mounted and turned her horse around. Anna grabbed Crisly around the waist, but before she could lift her onto the horse in front of her sister, she yelled, "Nay, wait!"

When Anna set her back down, she ran toward Scarface, pulled the weapon from his neck, and promptly spit on him before leaning down to wipe the knife clean on his clothes. His eyes stared at the sky, never moving. Crisly handed the knife to Anna and said, "We may need it again." To Anna's surprise, the lass ran back over to the young lad and nearly kicked him again, but she hesitated. "Sorry, but you cannot follow us. You're bad. Do you promise not to follow?"

The lad said, "I promise…" He rolled into a ball, clutching his belly. "I'll not try to stop you. Leave me be, please. I'll go back home and never do this again."

She couldn't help but wince for the lad. He was young and had possibly been forced to work with Scarface.

Once they were mounted, they turned the horses around and headed in the direction they'd come from.

Mariana shouted to her, "Do you remember how we got here?"

Anna said, "Do not worry. I'll lead the way." She prayed her memory would serve her well. She'd paid close attention to the landmarks they'd passed along the way.

"But how will you know which way to go? We were covered in the cart."

"I peeked." She winked at Marianna. "I memorized the flower trail on the way. I'll find our way back, but I think if we alter it a wee bit, we'll find ourselves closer to Drummond land."

They took off, not waiting to see if Scarface was truly dead or not, eager to simply get away.

"And my other advice? Follow the falcons if you see any."

CHAPTER SEVENTEEN

N O ONE IN THE HALL moved except Filib. "Mama? What are you saying?"

"Look what you've done, Jean. I told you…"

"Silence, MacGruder," the king ordered. "The truth needs to be told."

No one moved, waiting to hear the explanation for Jean MacGruder's outrageous claim.

David watched in shock as his mother pushed herself to standing and started across the room alone. Her voice came out in a whisper, but the cavernous room was so quiet that her every word was as clear as could be. "What are you saying, Jean?"

Tears poured down Jean's cheeks. "I loved your sire with all my heart, my lady. After he lost your dear mother, he was devastated. We met two years later and fell in love. He asked me to marry him, but I was already betrothed to Lorne. He would not release me from the betrothal, even though he knew I carried your sire's child."

A loud bellow came from the back of the room. Lorne. "And I have paid the price every day since then. How many times have I had to listen to you cry about how much you loved David Drummond? David Drummond… David Drummond. Then our daughter grows up and I must listen to the same thing. I don't wish to ever hear that evil name again! I only allowed this betrothal in the hopes our king or the Drummonds would award me some land…or at least some coin. I deserve it after everything the Drummonds have put me through, but nay. I was given naught." He turned to stare at King Alexander. "Naught!"

"And you'll still get naught, MacGruder," the king pronounced.

Lorne spun on his heel in a fury and headed toward the door.

Jean stared after her husband as he stormed out of the chamber. "He refused to let me go free. As for Filib, I never told your dear father, so do not blame him, my lady. But Lorne knew. I'd hoped to have a lass, but when it was a lad, he got me with child right away, and after I had Ossian, we switched the ages of the children. He would not allow his land to go to Filib."

She turned to Filib. "You are older than Ossian by a year. Your brother never knew you were a Drummond, but he always knew the truth about your ages. His sire told him you were older, but not why we switched your ages. His whole attitude changed after he discovered your true age. He always thought you would take away what he believed was rightfully his. It embittered him."

David's mother looked at Filib. "You're a Drummond, not a MacGruder." She spanned the remaining distance between them. "I have a brother. I know not how it makes you feel, but it pleases me." She kissed his cheek and stepped back, turning to King Alexander. "We will step out so they may have the chance to discuss this alone. We need to make plans to get Anna back."

The king nodded. "After careful consideration of the circumstances, my decree is that Anna shall be married to David. We will head back to the royal burgh at once. There are enough Ramsays here to see this marriage take place. Find the lass."

"Lorne didn't do it this time," Jean said, glancing at him from across the room. "I think Ossian did. Lorne lied about Ossian. We have not seen him since yesterday morn, so my husband sent Struan looking for him. He feared his secret would be uncovered. He likely thought the clans would never have reason to meet again if he got rid of Anna. 'Tis a sad truth, but I believe 'tis what happened."

Micheil asked, "Where is Struan?"

"He has not returned either."

Micheil said, "Then it could also be Struan, could it not?"

Jean's eyes teared up. "I suppose. He always had a soft spot for Ossian."

Diana led her group outside after the king took his leave. David made his way toward his parents, who were embracing.

"I'm proud of you, Diana," Micheil said. "You handled that news verra well."

"Aye, Mama, you did," David agreed.

She shrugged her shoulders. "I always wished for a brother or a sister. Now I have one, and he looks so much like Papa... I also wished for a daughter, but mayhap I'll have a granddaughter someday. I need a daughter-in-law first. Go find her, David. You must."

———◆———

ANNA, MARIANA, AND CRISLY CONTINUED on. She felt confident that they'd followed the correct path, but she wished to continue veering off toward Drummond land.

"Do you have any idea where the scarred man was holding us? I was not alert when I was taken. How far did you travel when you left your sire's land?" she asked Mariana.

"About two hours, I think."

"How far away was Drummond land from where you lived?"

"Papa said they were half a day away. He called it where the fortunate lived. We lived in a small group of four cottages, isolated in the woods. We worked the sparse bit of land together."

"You did? You planted food?"

Crisly nodded. "We did the rows together, and I had to weed. We grew nice turnips and we had big pea vines."

Their chatter stopped when Anna heard the call of a falcon. She looked overhead for the source, then Crisly pointed off into the distance. "Is that a falcon?"

"Why do you watch for falcons, Anna?" Mariana asked.

"You remember I told you about David's cousin Maggie? The one who found the bairns?"

"Aye."

"Her husband is known as the Wild Falconer. He has two falcons that follow him. So if you see a pair in the sky together, Will is probably not far." She slowed her horse to search the sky.

"Will they do whatever he tells them?"

"I'm not sure but keep your eye out for them. If you see two, we'll head in that direction."

Crisly shouted, "There. I see a smaller one over there."

She couldn't be sure, but she led them in that direction. "I think 'tis time to veer off toward the north. The falcons are in that direction, so mayhap we'll find David and his cousins sooner rather than later."

Out of nowhere came a lone horseman, headed directly for them. Her brother Ossian. He was riding much too fast for her to elude him.

Anna whirled to look at Mariana and Crisly. "I think 'tis my brother, and not the nice one. I can't outrun him with my mount. Promise me you'll search for the Drummonds. You have a chance." Her horse was a work horse, and a tired one at that. "Go. Now!"

She barely managed to finish her sentence before Ossian rode up alongside her, grabbing the reins of her horse and changing her direction.

"Ossian, nay. Leave me be! Go, Mariana. Go and don't stop."

Ossian's laughter echoed across the meadow they were

in. "Finally, I have you where I want you. You've put Papa through hell and I'm going to end it now. 'Tis only one way to be certain you'll not marry David Drummond. Papa may be afraid to do it, but not me."

Crisly clung to her sister's waist as they galloped away from her, but her eyes stayed on Anna.

"I have a lovely view from a waterfall to show you, Anna."

Afraid to ask what her brother had planned for her, she closed her eyes and thought of David. How she prayed they could find help before Ossian harmed her. Though she knew tricks to take down a full-grown man, if it came down to a contest of pure power, he would win.

———

DAVID WAS SURPRISED TO SEE his Grant cousins ride up as he was preparing to ready his mount and leave. "You got here quickly."

Connor nodded. "Your mother sent word to our family to prepare for assistance in a possible battle. She said you were not in need yet, but we were already headed to Nevin MacLerie's cottage to meet up with Will and Maggie. The messenger passed us on his way to Grant Castle. Once we caught up with him, we changed our destination at once. We're here to do all we can to help, though I'm sure my sire will ready our warriors. All you need to do is ask and they'll be on their way."

David was pleased to have the support of his cousins, but he was eager to leave as soon as possible. He gave everyone a brief explanation of what had transpired, making sure the Grants understood exactly what they were up against.

"Mayhap 'tis best if we split up," Connor said. "Braden, Roddy, and I can head north. Will and Maggie can head south, Gavin and Gregor east, and you can go west with your brother and Sweeney."

"Where is your brother?" Will asked.

David shook his head. "He was in the hall when the

news about Filib was revealed. But he disappeared right after Lorne MacGruder did."

A figure came barreling toward the group on horseback.

"Is that not your brother now?" Maggie asked, holding her hand up against the glare of the sun that had just peeked through the clouds.

David sighed. "Aye, 'tis Daniel."

"I'd say he knows something," Gavin said.

They didn't have to wait long. As soon as he was within speaking distance, Daniel shouted, "Ossian and Struan were just seen heading south. I know where they're going."

David decided not to ask how he'd found them so quickly. There was no time to waste.

"We're traveling together," Maggie announced.

Logan and Micheil came upon them just as they were leaving.

"Where are you all going together? Split up like you planned," Uncle Logan said.

"Nay, Daniel saw Ossian," David said.

Will held his arm up for one of the falcons, then sent him off to the south. "Where are we going, Daniel?"

"I heard them talking about hiding in a cave behind a waterfall. I know exactly where it is. Follow me."

David pulled his horse up next to Sweeney and whispered orders to him. The others were too busy asking Daniel questions to pay him any mind.

Sweeney grinned and nodded, "Aye, my lord. Consider it done." He took off in the opposite direction, whistling for two Drummond guards to accompany him.

David didn't wait for the others to get settled. He motioned for Daniel to lead the way and flicked the reins of his horse, moving into a fast gallop. He'd find that bastard and kill him for all the trouble he'd caused.

ANNA SCREAMED WHEN OSSIAN YANKED her off her horse about an hour later, throwing her to the ground. She scanned the area to see if she recognized it, but it wasn't familiar. They were in a small clearing among some trees, and she thought she heard the sound of falling water off in the distance. "Ossian, where are we?"

He bounded off his own horse and then pulled her to her feet, holding his dagger to her throat. "You don't need to know." He wouldn't even look at her. What had happened to her brother? He'd always had nasty tendencies, but this went far beyond any behavior she'd seen from him before.

Another horse came out of nowhere, and she prayed it would be someone who would help her. Her brother held onto her but lifted the dagger slightly from her throat once he saw it was her sire's second, Struan. A burst of hope lit her up inside.

"You shouldn't hurt her, Ossian," Struan said with a frown. "You'll limit your ability to bargain for what you want. Why aren't you in the caves like we discussed?"

The revelation that her father's second was against her too nearly caused her to lose her balance, but she hoped he could be reasoned with. "Struan, help me, please. Ossian is daft," she begged.

Ossian narrowed his gaze at Struan. "I no longer need your help. Whatever you want, leave. I'll take care of this myself." He tugged Anna behind him as he headed toward the sound of falling water.

Struan followed them. "Look, I agreed to help you get her away from the abbey so you could bargain for land from the Drummonds and some coin for me, but I'm not interested in killing anyone, especially not now that the king's around." The uncertainty in his voice was unsettling. He hadn't known her brother was going to act like this.

Ossian stopped and spun around to glare at Struan. "Papa gave me a job to do, and I plan to see it done. He said they cannot marry. Those were my instructions. I intend to get my lairdship when 'tis my time."

He started to drag her again, bringing her closer to what was beginning to sound like a waterfall.

"What the hell are you doing?" Struan said. "We agreed to hide her in the cave behind the falls and then go back to make our demands. Is the lass right? Have you truly gone daft?"

"I needed your help to get her out of the abbey yesterday, and I appreciate what you did, but I'll take over from here." He gave her a shove, pushing her ahead of him.

"My help? You'd never have been able to get her out alone. The monks wouldn't have trusted you enough to give you access to their chest of clothing. Nor could you have escorted her out yourself. 'Twas my knife aimed at her side that kept her in place."

"Aye, and for that I thank you. But I managed to get my wee sister back just fine on my own."

"Back? Where the hell has she been if not in the cave?"

"I sold her to the man connected with the Channel of Dubh yesterday. He paid some pretty coins for her. But then I decided 'twould be best to reclaim my bargaining chip. The king will likely demand to see her before he gives me what I want. So now I have her back and I'll hide her in the cave. Is that not what you want?"

"Aye, I'm glad you see it my way. We have to focus on our next steps. We'll leave her in the cave tied up, and after the Drummonds heed our demands, we'll reveal her location. They will give up land for her, I know they will. 'Tis an old way to deal for land, trading a body for more. 'Tis been done for decades in the Highlands. Our king knows of this practice."

"I'll get Drummond land and more. You'll see," Ossian said, stopping Anna and holding her close to him, tying her hands in front of her with rope.

"What the hell else do you want? You're heir to the

lairdship, and you just received coin for Anna. I don't know what you're planning, but I didn't agree to this." He stood next to them with his hands on his hips.

Ossian glanced up at the sky, squinting. "Nay, I guess you did not. Hold her for me, just for a moment, so I can explain." He pushed her toward Struan.

The older man grabbed her, and she couldn't help but appeal to him again. "Please, Struan, don't do this. Set me free." He was much taller than her, so he completely blocked her view of Ossian. She didn't care. Struan was the only one liable to help her. Something had gone badly wrong with Ossian. "Please help me," she begged. "He's gone mad!"

But he only tightened his grip on her hands.

She heard Ossian moving behind Struan, still jabbering. If she could kick Struan, perhaps she could run from Ossian, leap on the horse, and head north or...

Something in Struan's expression suddenly changed.

The man froze in place and his eyes widened. Then she noticed the tip of the sword protruding from his chest, blood pooling on his tunic. He let go of her hands and clutched his chest as he fell sideways. Terror pooled inside her. Had her brother just killed their sire's second in cold blood? Could she be next? Her hands began to tremble, and she wasn't sure if she'd ever be able to stop them.

Ossian stared up at the sky as though he had not a care in the world, his mind more twisted than Anna had ever suspected. "'Tis as I said, Struan," he said, "I don't need your help at all. I'll take care of it from here." He smiled as Struan's eyes took on a dull gaze. He twisted the dead man's body so he could pull his sword from his back.

Anna stared at her brother in shock. "Ossian, what have you done?" she asked, finally finding her voice. "How could you be so cold-hearted? He was Papa's second. He's been with us for years. Struan is dead!"

"I'll tell everyone you became daft and killed him." He

grabbed her arm and pushed her in front of him. "And you'll be next if you don't do what I ask."

CHAPTER EIGHTEEN

———◆———

THE BAND OF COUSINS TRAVELED for just over an hour when a horse approached them carrying two riders, young lassies. David held his sword up to signal his cousins and brother to stop.

The horse stopped in front of them. One girl was an adult, while the other looked to be around twelve summers. When they stopped, the elder of the two stared overhead at the circling falcons.

"The Wild Falconer...is he here? Are those your falcons?" the older girl asked in a shaking voice.

Will said, "Aye. How can I help you? Why are you two lasses traveling alone?"

"David Drummond?" the girl asked, glancing over the rest of the group.

"Aye," David replied. "What is it?"

She pointed back in the direction they'd just come from, her hand shaking. "Anna. Her brother stole her away. Said he was going to take her to a waterfall."

The wee lass added, "You must help her. She saved both of us." She looked terrified, but no more so than David felt. Had they come too late?

"Know you the area?" Maggie asked the group. "Where is this waterfall they speak of?"

Her comment helped David focus. A piece of him surged with pride. Anna had been the one to save the three of them from the Channel of Dubh? But the most important part of her message was that Anna was still in the area. That meant he could still save her. They had a chance.

"Aye. That way," Will and Gavin said in unison, pointing to the west. As soon as they spoke, he snapped to attention. He, too, knew the falls in this area. David started in that direction at once, but then stopped to glance at the lassies. They'd clearly been through an ordeal.

Maggie said, "I'll take care of them."

"Please don't send us back," the younger one said. "We have no home. Anna said you could help us."

Maggie waved the others on, and David heard her answer as he rode off.

"I was adopted into the Ramsay clan. We *will* find a place for you. Follow me."

He couldn't have said it better himself. Maggie, Molly, Simone, and three others had all been taken in by his uncle's clan. Anna had known to send them his way. He felt as though his chest were about to burst with pride.

Bringing his focus back to Anna, he set the pace toward the waterfall, his cousins fanning out around him. They made an impressive presence traveling in formation.

Only…one was missing.

Where the hell had Daniel gone off to now?

He had no time to look for his brother. He needed to make haste before Anna's captors did something horrible. Riding up to Gavin, he said, "I know the falls, but where should we leave our horses?"

"I know just the place. 'Tis not far from here," Will said. Less than an hour later, he stopped and led them over to a well-hidden spot, then whistled for his falcons, the peregrine arriving first and dropping down to sit on his shoulder while Stoirm, the Merlin, circled not far away.

The group of cousins gathered around David and Will as soon as they stopped. He nodded to Will, who seemed to know the area best from his time as a roaming wanderer, giving him leave to guide them. "Gavin and Gregor, in the trees with your arrows. This waterfall has a steep drop. The worst scenario is that he is wedged between the two trees just off to the right of the falls. He'll be hard to hit if he stands there with Anna in front of him, but it can be done from the right angle. There's another cliff next to that. If we need to, I can climb that and come at him from the trees above. If they're at the top, it's a steep drop into the gorge, lots of rocks. And be aware that Struan could be with him," he added.

"But the lasses said one man," Braden said.

"True. Struan hasn't come back yet, so 'tis a possibility he has an accomplice. I hope not but keep an open mind."

"Where would you like us?" Connor asked at once. Braden and Roddy stood beside him.

Will glanced at David, who said, "At the base of the falls. We know not what he plans. If he's lost his head, he could be attempting to drown her. You make your own judgment once we see where they are. I'll climb up the side, and if he's where I suspect he is, you can distract him from below or come at him from a different direction."

They went their separate ways. David headed toward the ravine but slowed when he noticed a body in the grass up ahead. He whistled for Will, who hadn't gone far.

"Who is it?" Will said.

David glanced at the body. "Struan, MacGruder's second. He's dead."

"Then we know who has Anna. Do you have any idea why Ossian would do this?"

David shrugged his shoulders. "Ossian fears he will lose the lairdship to his brother if anyone discovers the difference in their ages. He does not know Filib is my grandsire's son. Ossian likely thought he could hide the truth if he helped isolate the family."

"And killing is the only way?"

"I don't know why he had to kill Struan, unless he was trying to stop him for some reason."

Will shook his head. "Whatever his reasons, you need to finish this, Drummond. Get her back unharmed. He's unstable at the moment...unstable and desperate. I can't imagine his sire will be happy to discover his son has killed his second. I'll distract Ossian and you can climb."

They parted ways and David climbed up the side of the ravine, doing his best to listen to any sounds that could be heard over the rumbling of the water, forcing himself to focus on sounds and not to look down. He had issues with heights, though he'd been better about it of late. A scream carried to him that instantly froze him in his spot. There, wedged between two trees, Ossian stood with Anna in front of him, not far from the highest peak of the water-fall. They stood too close to the edge, and it was a long way down. He doubted Anna would survive a fall from that height. Will's worst-case scenario had come to pass. From the side, David could see how she trembled and that Ossian's hand was directly at her back, in the perfect position to give her a shove. He wisely used the trees to protect himself from arrows, so Gavin and Gregor were unlikely to have a clear shot. He had to move up.

Saving Anna could rest solely on his shoulders.

As if on cue, a whistle sounded from below and Will's two falcons circled and dove low into the water, the sight of them enough to unsettle anyone unfamiliar with Will's pets.

Ossian's voice carried over the water. "I know you're out there, Drummond. Come any closer and I'll shove her right over the edge."

To his surprise, Braden's voice carried across the water to him. "What do you want, MacGruder?"

"Who the hell are you?" Ossian shouted.

"Braden Grant. Whatever you want, I'll see you get it if you release the lass."

"A Grant?" Ossian chuckled. "From the renowned Grants of Dulnain Valley? Is Alex your sire? Aye, I'll deal with you. Here's what I want. Give me my own castle deep in the Highlands and I want one hundred guards."

Braden smirked. "Alex Grant is my uncle, but I'm from Clan Grant. Are you not going to ask for something difficult? Have you no idea how many warriors I have at my disposal as a Grant?"

"You'll see it done?" Ossian asked. "I know my sire will disinherit me now that I've killed his precious second, but both of them thought too small. If you give me my own land and promise to keep the king away from me, I'll set her free. I don't want the whore anyway. I've earned my coin from her."

"Let her go and we'll talk."

"Who's your sire?"

"Brodie Grant, brother to Alex."

"I want Alex Grant's guards. They're the best."

"You'll have them. I train them in the Grant lists every day. I can have my pick of the best warriors, and they'll do whatever I tell them to do. Let go of her and I'll come get her. Toss your weapon away."

Ossian chuckled. "I'm not that foolish. I think I'll keep her until we get deep into the Highlands. I'll come down, and we'll travel to Grant land together."

Will stepped out onto a rock in the middle of the water at the base of the falls. He held his arm out and Sealgar, the peregrine, swooped down and landed on his forearm. "If you don't set her free, I'll send this falcon up to peck your eyes out, MacGruder. You'll never make it to your horse. Let her go and I'll call my birds off."

"Leave Anna behind," Braden said soothingly, his patience a surprise. Of all the cousins, he was one of the most hot tempered. "She'll only slow us down. Meet me at your horse. Mayhap I'll join you in your new keep. I've had enough of the Grants, and methinks you and I can make something big in the Highlands. I can bring two hundred guards who answer only to us. But you have to let her go."

"Nay, I'm not letting her go. How can I know you're telling the truth?"

"You can't. You have to trust me. You don't like David Drummond? Well, neither do I. He's just like my cousin Connor. Everyone will look up to them just because of who their sires are. Me? Naught has been handed to me. You and I could control our own castle, have our own warriors. *We* could be in control."

"Why are you here, Grant?" Ossian asked.

"I came for a wedding, but I'd gladly form an alliance with you. 'Tis time for me to grow up, to make a stand on my own."

David had to smirk at Braden's seemingly heartfelt offer. He knew how much Braden loved his cousins—besides which, he'd actually heard the man say he didn't want to be a laird. Too much responsibility. He was baiting Ossian, and how he hoped the fool would take the bait. He glanced down at Braden, just now realizing how far he'd climbed. He had to promise himself not to look down again. The drop was quite steep.

Gavin appeared on a rock not far away, pulling his bow out and nocking an arrow. "You're in my line of sight, MacGruder. Let her go."

David continued to climb, hoping his cousins kept the distraction up. *Don't look down, don't look down. Do this for Anna.* Sweat broke out across his forehead, but he ignored it. If he could come up on the side of Ossian, he'd strike him dead. He'd just have to do it with the utmost care because Anna was on the edge. He had ascended another several feet when another voice rang out from a spot on his side of the ravine.

"You're in my direct line of sight, too," Gregor said. "If you lose him, Gavin, I've got him."

David glanced up in time to see Ossian's gaze dart from one cousin to the other and back to Will and Braden, still standing with the falcon poised on his arm. To his surprise, he saw Roddy and Connor climbing directly up the falls, out of Ossian's line of sight.

Will asked, "Have you met my other falcon yet, Mac-Gruder? He loves to travel in these parts. I could call him to greet you if you don't do as we ask."

"Call him off me, Grant," Ossian said. "No falcons. Do it or I'll toss her over the edge."

David's gut clenched in reaction, making him hurry as best he could.

"Will, no falcons," Braden said, "or I'll use my arrow to take one out. Do as I say." Braden pulled out his bow and arrow, aiming it at the sky to emphasize his threat.

Will held his arm out and the smaller falcon hovered over his shoulder before finally alighting. "You win, Grant. I'll call them both off." Sealgar hadn't left him yet.

"You're smarter than I thought, Grant. Make sure he keeps those falcons there, or I'll push Anna. I've heard stories about those vicious birds. I heard they pecked a man's neck until he bled out. Keep them down there. If I go, she goes with me."

"No reason to hurt a lass," Braden said. "Nor should we let her slow our journey. Why, we could be well on our way in a matter of hours. I know all the paths."

Ossian thought for a moment. David prayed it would be a long moment. He was almost there.

Ossian said, "Nay, she goes with us."

He glanced down in time to see Will wave his arms to send both falcons straight toward Ossian and Anna.

CHAPTER NINETEEN

ANNA PULLED STRENGTH FROM DEEP in her belly to squelch her scream. The falcons soared into the air and dropped down right near them, one in front of her and one behind her.

Ossian was not ruffled at all.

"I hardly think a bird can push me over the edge. I, however, can easily push this lass over the edge."

He turned to glance at Anna. "Seems they all lie for you, even a Grant."

He pushed his shoulder into her back, but she had grabbed the trunk of the small tree and wrapped her arm around it. She screamed, and just as she did, an arrow sluiced through the air, barely missing them. She ducked her head in anticipation of a second arrow, and one came from the opposite direction.

How she prayed it would hit Ossian.

"Ossian, please," she said desperately. "I'll not cause you any trouble. I'll just marry David and live on Drummond land. Why are you doing this? I don't understand."

Another arrow flew by them and he cursed. "Because now I have to leave. Struan got in the way. My sire will never give the land to me now. He'll give it to Filib because he's older than me. I have to go on the run, and heading deeper into the Highlands sounds good to me. Mayhap I'll take my warriors on a ship and head to the land of the Norse. Do you like galley ships, sister?"

Anna couldn't follow what Ossian had said about their ages. "What? You're older than Filib." The falcon swooped down and brushed Ossian's shoulder, forcing him backward. For a moment, Anna lost her bearings, and when she looked down at the long drop she'd face if she ever let go of the tree, her knees went weak.

"Filib is the eldest. Papa switched us because he never liked Filib. But now that I killed his precious Struan, he'll give it to Filib. I have to escape or they'll hang me. You're my only chance to get away, so you go with me, or we both go over the edge. What's your answer?"

He ducked from another arrow, then grasped her arm, yanking it free of the tree, but she grabbed it in another spot. "On second thought, this could work better. I'll just throw you over the edge. That will distract them all and I can run to my horse. Good-bye, dear sister."

He pinched her fingers open until she let go of the tree, then shoved her forward. She grasped at an overhanging branch just as a deep growl came from off to the side.

David threw himself at Ossian, knocking him to the ground and forcing him away from Anna. He threw three or four punches before he jumped to his feet and stood back, grabbing the hilt of his sword just as Ossian went for his own weapon and charged toward him. Anna screamed, but David easily blocked his thrust. They parried, grunting, slamming metal against metal, sweat and dirt flying everywhere.

She hid her face once she found her way back to the tree, so afraid David would be hurt in front of her eyes. When she dared, she peeked again in time to see David plunge his sword into Ossian's belly.

Her brother stared at David in shock, clutching his wound once David pulled his sword free. Gasping for air, David turned to her and she launched herself at him, throwing her arms around his neck and burying her face in his chest.

"Hush, I have you, sweet. 'Tis over. Everything is over. We'll be together forever." He stood back and grasped her chin, turning her face from side to side as the tears ran down her cheeks. "Did he hurt you?"

She shook her head, unable to get any words out, instead falling into his chest again, sobbing. "I knew he hated me, but I don't understand why he did this."

"Hush, I'll explain later." He cupped her cheeks and kissed her, a deep kiss that told her how much he loved her. When he tried to pull back after a while, she tugged him closer instead, dipping her tongue inside his mouth. How she loved him.

Could she be so fortunate to have this nightmare ended?

A strange sound caught them both, interrupting their sweet embrace, and David immediately pushed her behind him.

Ossian had managed to stand and was headed directly toward them, his arms outstretched and ready to shove.

A body dropped out of the tree behind Ossian and gave him a shove, forcing him over the falls, plunging to his certain death.

"Hellfire, Daniel. Where did you come from?" David asked in disbelief. "What the hell are you, a ghost?"

Daniel grinned and pointed to the branches above. "You really shouldn't allow yourself to be so distracted at times like these." He took off toward his cousins at the bottom of the falls, the hooting and hollering of their celebration carrying to them over the pounding of the water against the rocks below.

Anna was so relieved she fell against David and squealed. "Is it finally over? May we leave now?"

"Gladly, since I'm not overly fond of heights. Just looking over the edge makes me queasy." He kissed her lips, just a soft kiss of surrender. "Aye. 'Tis time to take our leave."

He helped her down the back way, which was a longer trek, but safer for her. She was glad of it.

"I met two friends, David. We have to invite them to join the Drummonds if your mama agrees. Mariana and Crisly."

"We met them. They told us you were being taken to the waterfall, or we would have had no idea where to find you. Fortunately, Will, Gavin, and I knew of this area. Maggie took the lasses back to the abbey. Where did you meet them?"

He led the way down the steep embankment slowly, being careful to stand in front of her in case she lost her footing. Dear David always thought of everything.

She glanced at the man she loved. The last thing she wished to think about was Scarface and what she'd done to him. "I'll tell you later. What matters is that you found me."

"Lass, I'm sorry about your brother."

She stared at the ground, pausing for a moment. "I suppose I should be, but I'm not. There was always something evil inside Ossian. Watching him up there was verra frightening."

By the time they made it back to their horse, everyone had left except for Daniel.

David asked, "Where'd they go, Daniel? I enjoyed riding with them. We look impressive together, do we not?"

"They went ahead to give you and Anna space. I'm not nearly as thoughtful. I'll ride with you and help lead the way."

Before Anna mounted, she turned to David and whispered, "Will we be able to marry?"

He kissed her cheek and said, "Do not worry. I've taken care of everything."

Anna sighed and leaned back against him as they headed back toward the abbey. When had she ever been so happy?

CHAPTER TWENTY

THE DAY HAD TURNED OUT to be glorious. Anna turned her face up to the Highland breeze, then leaned back against David. His hand went to the back of her neck, softly massaging her tender skin. After all that had happened, what would become of her family?

Anna felt a strong wish to see her mother, and she hoped Filib was waiting for her, too. Did they know Ossian was now dead? And Struan? What would her sire think?

When they arrived at the abbey, David and Anna were escorted to the door to be certain there were no interruptions this time.

Had everyone heard of her troubles?

She gripped David's hand as they stepped inside. The abbess welcomed the two of them back, though the look on her face indicated she certainly had not forgotten the other evening. She then led them down the passageway to a chamber, opening the door and closing it behind them.

Anna's mother and Filib sat close together at a small table, both of them looking anxious and mournful. As soon as Anna stepped into the room, her mother leaped to her feet and rushed to her side. "You are hale and hearty? I was so worried."

"Aye, Mama, and I'm unhurt thanks to David and his cousins. Where is Papa? I don't know if you've heard yet, but I'm sorry to tell you that Ossian is dead. He killed Struan and then tried to kill me. He brought it on himself."

Her mother stared at her, not saying a word, such a shocked look on her face, Anna feared she might faint. She paled and reached out to grab her mother's hand, but Filib came up behind her.

Filib said, "Mama, sit down." They settled the poor woman in a chair, and Anna moved to sit next to her.

Her mother gripped her hand and whispered, "I'm so sorry. I fear this could be my fault. I fear…"

Anna had no idea what her mother was talking about, but perhaps the entire day had simply been too much for her. "Mama, do not be ridiculous. None of this is your fault. My rape was a fraud. Papa paid a man to knock me out and make it appear as if I'd been attacked. Ossian sold me to a man who planned to send me on a cargo ship to the East. For some odd reason, he believed he needed to get rid of me."

Her mother gasped, tears misting her eyes. "Oh dear. How awful. What if David hadn't saved you? A cargo ship to the East? Why? What…?" She paled and her hand came up to her mouth. "Nay, tell me it cannot be true. My dear daughter. How could he have done this to you? David, you have my deepest gratitude. Anna, your father will be in shock to hear about Ossian. He never intended for everything to go that far…"

"Mama, where is Papa?"

"Your father took his guards and headed home, though he sent five guards off to find Struan. I never liked that man. I don't understand any of this. Why would Ossian try to sell you?"

David squeezed Anna's hand and said, "Allow me. Ossian sold her for the coin, but he then changed his mind. He told Anna he feared he would be switched with Filib again. That the truth about their ages would come out and be used against him."

Her mother looked up at her, a pained expression on her face. "You knew?"

"Aye. Ossian told me about switching their ages, but why?"

Her mother grasped her hand and said, "I need to tell you something. Lorne is not Filib's sire. His sire is David Drummond, your husband's grandsire."

Anna was stunned. She glanced at David, who nodded in affirmation. "She told us all when you were missing. It was a difficult thing for her to do, but it helped us find you. There was no time to explain before."

She listened, her hand clasped tightly in David's as her mother explained everything. She then turned her attention to Filib. "But that makes you…"

Filib smiled. "I'm still your half-brother, but I'm a Drummond. Your husband is my nephew, I suppose."

Her mother's expression was still confused. "But if Ossian sold you, why were you with him?"

David took over the tale again. "Ossian pocketed the coin from selling Anna, but then had apparently planned something with Struan."

Filib said, "Aye. We discovered Struan obtained the monks' clothing to get Anna out."

Anna did her best to explain what she'd heard. "Struan and Ossian had planned to kidnap me, hide me in a cave, and ransom me for land from the Drummonds and coin. Papa felt he deserved it, and they were doing it for Papa. But Ossian saw the opportunity for more coin once he had me away from the abbey so he sold me to the man in the Channel, then returned to steal me back to use as a bargaining chip. The only part of it Struan agreed to was hiding me in a cave and trading me for land. But for some reason he killed Struan. Then I knew he'd gone completely daft. Poor Struan."

Her mother shook her head slowly, her jaw opening wider as the details were revealed.

"How did Ossian die?" Filib asked.

"He tried to push me over the edge," Anna said. "But

David stopped him. He pulled a knife on David, and David killed him with his sword. I'm sorry, Mama."

"Or I thought I killed him. He managed to get to his feet and charged toward us, but my brother pushed him over the edge of the falls. 'Tis where his body landed, though the water may have taken him downstream."

"Don't be sorry," she said with a hoarse voice. "I loved him because he was my son, but I know his soul was twisted."

A knock sounded at the door. Diana stuck her head inside and said, "May I come in?"

Anna glanced at her mother to see how she felt about it, and to her surprise, her mama was waving Diana inside.

Diana entered, Micheil Ramsay following fast behind her. "I'm sorry that all this has disrupted your wedding day," Diana said, "but I hope the tragedies are over for now." She turned her attention to Filib. "I'm not sure how you feel, but I'd like to get to know you better, so I'm inviting you to come and spend a fortnight at Drummond Castle. I'll tell you more about our father. I know he would want me to do so, and I hope you'll accept."

Filib thought it over for a moment and then nodded. "I would like that. I don't think I'll be welcome on Mac-Gruder land any more. I can find my own way, but I would like to know more about my true sire. Mama, what are you going to do?"

She smiled and Anna was struck by her expression. The sadness was still there, but it seemed to coexist with a more enduring contentment. "You may find this odd, but I feel so...*free*. I no longer have to carry this lie around with me. For now, I'd like to spend some time here at the abbey. I held many secrets over the years. I did what I thought was best, but it ended up hurting you both. It seems inadequate, but all I can do is apologize. I told Lorne that your betrothal would be for the best, even knowing how he felt. Struan and I both convinced him he could gain land or something from the alliance. I was wrong, and for my part in this, I need to get closer to the Lord. I'm sure I can find some work to do here. I'll not be returning to Lorne, but I hope you will both visit me on occasion." Tears misted her eyes and she whispered, "I do love you both." She kissed Anna's cheek and then Filib's. "Anna, I so hope you will be happy. I wanted you to marry David all along, but your sire is a stubborn man."

"Oh, Mama. David and I will be back to visit."

"I hope you do, but 'tis time for you to begin your life together."

Diana cleared her throat. "Anna, there are two people outside this room who are anxious to see you and David, may I bring them in?"

Anna glanced at David before nodding. She had no idea who Diana meant, but she knew she trusted her. Diana opened the door and Crisly came charging across the floor, running straight for Anna. Mariana followed behind her.

Crisly wrapped her arms around Anna's waist and cried, "I was so worried about you. You are the strongest lass I've ever met, but when I saw him kidnap you, I wanted to cry."

Anna hugged her back, feeling tears well in her eyes. "David, this is Mariana and her sister Crisly. They helped me to escape."

Mariana said, "The only one who helped was Crisly. She stole the knife and then gave it to Anna. It was Anna who tricked Scarface into coming up close enough for her to stab him in the neck."

Crisly said, "Blood was everywhere. I've never seen aught like that."

Her mother gasped, and David's jaw dropped open. "Anna? Is this true?"

He glanced at his mother, who was beaming with pride. Anna sat up a bit taller and said, "Aye, 'tis true."

For a moment, she was worried about how he would react, but David leaned in to kiss her cheek. "I'm so proud of you," he said. "Had you not done that, I shudder to think what would have happened."

Crisly shouted, "We could have been on a ship now, headed for some unknown place."

"We told Maggie, Will, and her sire everything we knew about the Channel of Dubh," Mariana said. "Maggie said they'd find a way to put an end to it so no one would ever fall victim to them again."

Crisly said, "Aye, 'twas almost terrible for us, but now we're being adopted into a new family." She clapped her hands together, her enthusiasm and excitement contagious.

Anna couldn't be happier. "You are? Who is adopting you?"

Diana came up behind the two of them and gave them a squeeze. "We are. David, meet your new sisters. 'Twas an easy decision. I've always wanted a daughter. Now I have two."

Anna broke into laughter over the thought of having the two as sisters-in-law. Before they were done, she had the entire group laughing along with her, even her mother. "Oh, Mama. 'Tis good to see you laugh again."

A knock sounded at the door, and when David answered it, Daniel stood there, his usual grin on his face. "We're ready for you two."

Anna glanced at David, perplexed. "For what?"

David stood and held his hand out to her. "Anna Mac-Gruder, will you marry me, right now? I'll not be kept waiting any longer."

She jumped up and threw her arms around his neck. His mother said, "Not yet. You must follow the trail first."

Anna's gaze traveled from one person to the next. "The trail?"

David extended his hand to her. "Come with me, love. I asked Sweeney to do me a favor, but this will be a surprise for me as well."

Anna glanced at David. "Where are we going?"

"It would seem 'tis a secret. We'll just have to wait." David tugged her into the passageway, following Daniel outside.

Where were they headed?

———◆———

DAVID GLANCED AT DANIEL, WHO simply grinned. He wondered what his brother had planned. All he'd asked Sweeney to do was find a priest and some flowers for Anna so they could still marry today. Daniel had something unusual planned for sure.

He followed his brother outside, holding Anna's hand. Daniel led them to a horse with ribbons tied to its tail and flowers entwined in its mane. Anna squeezed David's hand, telling him how much she approved of the horse they were to ride. His brother mounted his own horse and held his hand out, indicating they should mount up. He noticed his father and mother were behind them, along with Anna's mother and Filib, all on horseback.

"Allow me, wife-to-be. 'Tis time for us to marry." He helped her mount the horse and climbed up behind her. His brother led them through a dense grouping of trees. When they came through the other side, they were greeted by a sight more pleasing than he'd guessed he would ever see. He lifted Anna's chin and turned her face forward. "Look, my sweet."

From the opposite side of the meadow, a small group of Grant guards bedecked in their red plaids approached David and Daniel, Connor in the lead, bellowing the Grant war whoop. Braden approached them with another group.

"Follow me," Daniel said. "I've got it all set up. I was worried the MacGruder warriors might decide to come along and try to stop us, so we've arranged an escort for you. The wedding could have been held at the abbey, but I feared it might not have the best memories for Anna. We thought this would work better. You both deserve something special—and what could be more special than marrying in front of our extended family and allies?"

David followed his brother, shocked that he'd had the foresight to make such arrangements. Connor fell in behind them as Roddy's warriors came along one side of them and Braden's warriors protecting his other side.

The Grant warriors began to fall back as another slew of warriors approached them from the front, Ramsay warriors in their blue plaids circled them, Gavin and Gregor whooping the Ramsay shout for all to hear.

Anna peeked at him, excitement bubbling out of her. He leaned down and whispered in her ear. "Believe me when I say 'tis over. You'll be my wife soon."

They didn't travel far before another slew of warriors joined them. The Drummonds, bedecked in their red and black plaids, surrounded them completely. David's parents joined the warriors and rode alongside them.

"Where are you taking us, Daniel?"

Daniel let out his own Drummond war whoop and charged his horse forward. Will and Maggie, who had been riding with the Ramsays, fell in next to them, all smiles.

David glanced over his shoulder, so impressed with the sight that a lump formed in his throat. A sea of warriors escorted them forward, protecting them as they traveled to their unknown destination. His Band of Cousins had fallen in directly behind him.

Anna pointed off into the distance. Lorne MacGruder sat on his horse a short distance away with several of his guards. He just stared at the procession flying past him, his shoulders slumped in resignation.

He'd lost his daughter and his son.

David nudged Anna and pointed to something. Mariana and Crisly rode with the Drummonds, huge smiles on their faces.

The cavalry slowed as another two horses approached David and Anna. Daniel motioned for them to move forward, toward the newcomers, and his cousins made a tight circle around them.

Sweeney sat on one horse, grinning from ear to ear. Father Rab, the Ramsay priest, rode the other horse.

Daniel held his sword up to silence everyone, and Sweeney said, "I hope you're accepting of the idea of being married on horseback."

"Well done, Daniel, Sweeney," David said with a grin, turning to look at Anna. Her smile was just as wide, so he said, "I think my bride-to-be will agree."

"Wait!" Sweeney drew close and handed a small sack to David. He opened the bag and pulled out a beautiful bouquet of fresh flowers tied together, full of purple, yellow, and white blossoms.

David handed the bouquet to Anna and whispered, "Will this suit you, love?"

She nodded enthusiastically. Father Rab directed everyone where he wanted them, though he had to interrupt David's sire and his brothers at least twice before they heeded him. They were looking over the Band of Cousins with pride, jesting about which cousin was best. Uncle Quade, the eldest and most level headed of the brothers, said, "Shut up, you two, and listen."

Father Rab nodded to Quade. "My thanks. Do we have a Drummond plaid available?"

David's mother came forward, handing over the Drummond dress plaid, while his father came around to their other side.

Father Rab rode closer to the couple and wrapped their hands together, entwining the fabric around and between them, reciting in Gaelic all the while.

David glanced at Anna, her face alight with happiness, her eyes brimming with unshed tears. Their moment had finally come, and he was so overwrought with emotion and love, he barely heard any of the words Father Rab said. Their love was so worth fighting for, their love was true, and they'd have their own bairns someday.

When Father Rab declared them husband and wife, David cupped her cheeks and settled his lips on hers, tasting her happiness if that were possible. When they ended the kiss, Anna broke out in a giggle and pointed to the Band of Cousins, now running their horses in a circle around them while the elders had moved back, allowing them this simple celebration of their marriage.

David's parents and Anna's mother and brother joined in Anna's laughter and offered their congratulations.

They were finally husband and wife.

CHAPTER TWENTY-ONE

———◆———

WHEN THEY FINALLY STOPPED THEIR horses, David wasn't sure what to expect. Where would they go to spend their first night together?

Anna whispered, "What now? Are we going to Drummond Castle?"

"I'm not sure," David said. He pulled his horse next to his brother and Sweeney. "Many thanks to both of you for planning this."

His cousins stopped and gathered around them. "Congratulations," Will said, followed by a chorus of the same.

"Our thanks," David said, his hand on Anna's waist. "We cannot express how much we appreciate all you did for us."

Anna nodded. "Thank you all."

David's mother came forward with her horse, broke into the middle of the group of cousins, and gestured for them to follow her. "Follow me."

After several rounds of good-natured goodbyes, they left and followed Diana. They rode for about half an hour before she led them off the regular path, deeper into the forest until they could hear the rumble of a small waterfall not far away. When they could go no farther, she stopped and dismounted. "Your aunt and uncle couldn't get here in time, but they sent a missive saying you're welcome to use their favorite home away from their castle."

"Another aunt and uncle?" Anna asked.

"Aye, David's Aunt Avelina, Micheil's only sister, and her husband, Drew. They had this built a while ago. She's verra connected to nature, so it was a gift from Drew."

She motioned for them to dismount, grabbed her saddlebag, and then led the way through the forest.

"Anna, I've heard about your love for flowers. I don't know how you feel about faeries, but Avelina believes that flowers make them verra happy. She has a special connection with the faeries, which I'm sure David will explain to you sometime. She and Drew like to come here on occasion to remember how their relationship started. Come with me. We shall have to walk the rest of the way."

She led them down a long path. They traveled deep into the woods, and the deeper they went, the more the flowers blossomed around them.

There was a thick covering of moss over many of the rocks, decorated with pink-colored star flowers that were absolutely beautiful. Then they passed a large grouping of bluebells aimed at the sun.

"These are some of my favorites," Anna said with a gasp. "I love bluebells this time of the year." She bent down to pick a couple and added them to her bouquet that she still held.

"Aunt Avelina considers bluebells to be faerie flowers. She loves them. She has done her best to transplant more down this path. And this one is *Biolair ghriagain,*" she said, pointing to a beautiful white flower, "'tis another one of her favorites."

David leaned down and whispered, "This looks like your dream home, Anna. Flowers everywhere."

Anna took in everything as they walked, her eyes jumping from bush to flower to the birds overhead singing their delight. Finally, his mother stopped. "Welcome to the wee faerie castle."

The area was small and private, full of large trees and abundant wildflowers. A small cottage sat on a small knoll at the edge of a spring near the base of a short waterfall. There was a plethora of flat rocks around the water, perfect to relax on.

"When the sun is high, there is naught more luxurious than taking a dip in the water and drying out on the rocks. No one will bother you, I promise," his sire said, his voice bursting out from behind them, surprising them all. "My sister loves it here. She's so happy to be able to share it with you two." He wrapped his arm around his wife. "Sorry it took me a while to catch up with you. Getting my brothers to do aught at all is most difficult."

The couple led them inside the cottage. "There are only two rooms," Diana said. "We brought bread, cheese, and fruits, so you likely won't need to cook on the hearth. Your sire found a bottle of wine he'd been saving and brought it along with two goblets, David, and we added a jug of mead." She opened her saddlebags and brought out the goblets while Micheil produced the jug. "I also brought a satchel of extra clothing for both of you so you can swim."

She led them into the second room. An enormous bed draped with canopies and piled with soft, pastel-colored pillows filled the chamber.

"Oh my," Anna said, "I've not seen one that large before. And look at all the pillows! It looks divine. Many thanks to you both."

His father clasped David's shoulder. "So proud of both of you. We wish you much happiness. I doubt you'll be in need of aught. We've tried to think of everything possible. Feel free to stay as long as you like, but I'm sure your mother will come searching for you if she hasn't heard from you after three or four days, David."

They thanked his parents profusely and waved goodbye to them. After they left, he and Anna stood outside staring at the beautiful glen, hand in hand, when something caught his eye. "Is that steam coming from the water?"

Anna's eyes glimmered with excitement. She promptly

removed her boot and walked over to the edge of the small pool to stick her toe into the water. "Oh, David." She closed her eyes, sighing with pleasure. "The water is quite warm. I'm going in now."

David watched in surprise as his wife tossed her clothing off to the side without a shred of embarrassment. Her moan of pleasure when she stepped into the water was motivation enough for him to strip out of his own clothes, in record timing, and follow her.

"Anna, och, you're so bold."

She gave him a saucy look and said, "Do you mind?"

"Nay," he growled, grabbing her and pulling her close for a kiss. He kissed her hard, letting her know how much he wanted her, remembering how it had felt to be inside her. "Now I have you all to myself, lass. I will know every last area of your body, and I promise to make you scream my name with pleasure." He couldn't stop himself from running his hands down her beautiful curves.

"I could already scream your name with pleasure, just being beside you in this warm water. I need to sink into this completely." She fluttered her lashes at him.

"You don't understand my meaning, I see. Allow me to show you."

"David, let me languish in the warmth of the water for a couple of moments first. Please?" She gave him a sassy grin that told him she was as interested in their lovemaking as he was, so he could hardly turn such a request down. A few moments later, he was pleased he'd given in to her.

They slipped into the warm pool together, sliding down until their shoulders were covered. "Anna, is it possible all these events have changed you as they have me? There was a time when you were timid, even though you kissed me first. You were timid around your family."

She leaned back, allowing the warm water to surround her as she lifted her feet so she could float freely. "Was I? Perhaps you are right. Being around my sire and Ossian was intimidating. I've never felt that way around you. Mayhap 'tis you that has changed me. I am more confident around you. How have you changed?"

He gazed up at the clouds, one eye closed. "Having the confidence to stand up for what I believe in. At first, when your sire said the betrothal was canceled, I thought there was naught I could do to stop him. My cousins helped me to realize we were strong together. That if I wanted something badly enough, I would find a way to make it happen. I know I've surprised my parents." He couldn't help but chuckle. "My sire even asked me when I grew up. Something like that."

"David, no one else could understand our love. 'Tis meant to be. We both knew it and were not about to allow anyone else to put our love asunder." She floated closer to him and kissed his shoulder as he sat in the water. "Now that I know what happened to my poor mother, I'm so glad we fought for each other."

"Aye, my grandpapa and your mother. Is that not strange?"

"Most strange. Do you remember him at all? Do you look like him?"

"Nay, I don't remember him," he said wistfully. "He died before I was born. They say he was a character but also a fine laird. Do I look like him? I'll have to ask my mother that question."

"There were some surprises, were there not?" she arched her brow at him. "Could you believe it when I was betrothed to Gilroy Walters?"

"Nay," he growled. "Never mention that name again, though I'm sure he's gravely disappointed."

"I'm still surprised my mother stood up against my sire."

He reached for her hips under the water and tugged her back against him. "Aye, but there was one event that surprised me more than anything. Had I still held any idea you were timid, I would have lost it when you begged me to take your maidenhead in the abbey." He gave her a glance full of confusion, his lips twisted in an odd way. "I never would have believed it. In the abbey, no less."

Anna began to laugh, throwing her head back with glee, and before he knew it, they were both laughing hysterically over everything that had happened. She managed to get out between her chuckles, "I know this is wrong after we've been through so many tragedies, but it feels so good to laugh."

He ran his hands up her thighs, and as soon as his laughter calmed, he turned her around to face him and pulled her close for a kiss. "Wife, I'm thrilled to see you laugh. I thought we'd never share such pleasure again."

She whispered, "But I always believed in us, David. I always believed you'd come for me."

"And you were right." He released her, and she dropped her shoulders underneath the water.

"I like it better under the water. Come with me."

The strain in his cock forced him to say something else. "I'd prefer to watch you instead. Just for a few moments. You are so beautiful. Allow me this simple pleasure."

She giggled. "As you wish, my lord." She rolled onto her back in the water, tipping her head back and closing her eyes to the sun, her breasts bobbing in the heat, brazenly pointing her rosy nipples up to the sky. He had to fist his hands at his side to keep from reaching out to her.

"Do you have any idea how much you taunt me, wife?"

"I thought you wished to watch me."

"I can only watch for so long before I need to touch you." He gritted his teeth as the water rolled across her body.

She opened her eyes and glanced at him, then looked at her body floating in the early sun. "The heat feels wonderful, David. I won't torture you. Feel free to touch me."

He moved forward boldly, bringing his hand straight to the center of her belly before tracing a careful path up to her breasts, slowly kneading each proud mound, tweaking her nipples until she moaned.

Her eyes closed, her small moan going straight to his cock. "That feels wonderful. I had no idea marriage could be so enjoyable."

"Your breasts are begging for my attention, floating atop the water the way they do."

His hand grazed down her center, careful not to put any pressure on her so he wouldn't submerge her. He was enjoying the view of her gorgeous body.

In fact, he was quite certain he could watch her forever.

He moved between her legs, gently maneuvering her ankles so she was in the right position for him, and caressed a path up the inside of each thigh until his hands met in the center of her curls. She lifted her head to stare at him, her heavy-lidded gaze teasing his cock more than the sensation of her soft skin beneath his fingers. He wrapped his arms around her knees and tugged her closer until he dropped his head to her mound, his tongue flicking out to catch her nub.

She squealed and squirmed in the water. "David, what are you doing?"

"Getting to know you. 'Tis what I promised, and I'm a man of my word." He lowered his shoulders into the water and brought her closer, his tongue caressing every part of her. He licked and suckled until she moaned, a sweet sound that could nearly drive him to the edge.

"David, I think I might drown." Her arms flailed as she struggled to keep her head above water.

He pushed her forward until her back met a rock at the side of the pool. Placing his hands on her bottom, he lifted her, caressing her folds before he set her on the rock, pulling her over to the edge so he could finish what he had started.

"Lean back, love. I need to be inside you, but not until I finish this."

She gazed at him, the trust in her eyes humbling. "Please don't stop." She did as he suggested and leaned back on her elbows.

He used his tongue to tease her again until she opened wide for him. He entered her with his finger then, keeping his tongue on her pleasure spot while he moved inside her in a rhythm he hoped would bring her to climax.

"Come for me, Anna," he whispered, continuing his ministrations.

"Oh, David!"

He took her nub in his mouth and suckled hard until she cried out, her contractions tightening around his finger.

She fell back panting on the rocks, and all she could say was, "Oh my."

He couldn't wait any longer. "I know you'd like to lie back and enjoy the sensations, but I'm about to lose myself after watching you." He reached for her hands and tugged her to a sitting position before he helped her slide back into the water.

His mouth descended on hers and he ravaged her, tasting every corner of her sweet mouth, relishing every touch of her tongue.

He could wait no longer. He lifted her and slid into her with a groan, pleased to find she was still slick with juices to welcome him. He settled one hand on the rock behind her back, the other holding her bottom close to him, and plunged into her, suddenly unable to control his need. His mouth dropped to her breast and he took the full weight of her into his mouth, her soft cries driving his need to even greater heights.

Her hands found their way into his hair, and she tugged him closer. He let go of her breast to focus his attention on her nipple, suckling and grazing his teeth across the tip as he sensed her nearing another climax.

He drove into her over and over again, panting with a need, her own voracious appetite pushing him to take her harder, faster, deeper. They clung to each other, the sound of water slapping between them, her own pants echoing in his ear.

"I love you, David."

Her contractions squeezed him as she screamed his name, forcing him over the edge to his own release, pouring his seed into her with a growl. His orgasm rocked him to his core, and all he could think about was how wonderful they were together, how loving this woman would make him happy for the rest of his days.

How finally, after everything they'd been through, they were together. Just as they should be.

She fell limp against him and he cuddled her to him, stroking her back as they fought to control their panting.

"I have something for you, my sweet," David whispered when he was able to control his breathing. He let go of her and moved over to the edge where he'd dropped his plaid, reaching across a stone for his sporran. He reached inside until he grasped the delicate chain of the necklace, pulling it out to hold it up for her. "For you."

The excitement in her gaze made his trip to Edinburgh worth it. He'd almost forgotten that he had it, so caught up in the chaos of their wedding day, but he'd carried it in his sporran for days. "My wedding gift to you."

"Oh, David," she purred, holding the palm of her hand out to him so he could drop the necklace inside. She fingered the pendant and said, "I believe 'tis the most beautiful necklace I've ever seen. A white rose. It almost looks like the white flower I saw on the path we came through. 'Twill be a symbol of our love." She stood on the tips of her toes and kissed him softly on his lips. "My thanks, husband. I love it and will wear it always." She turned her back to him and handed him the necklace so he could fix the clasp for her. As soon as it fell against her neck, her fingers reached up to caress the rose. She spun around to look at him, a wide smile on her face.

Surprising him yet again, she wrapped her legs around his middle and then interlocked her hands with his, pushing him away from the rock enough for her to fall back lazily into the water. "How does it look in the water?"

"Not as lovely as you." He couldn't help but smile as he watched her bask in the water. He leaned over and kissed her navel. "I do love you, Anna. But you know that, I'm certain. Did I please you?"

When she was finally able to speak, she whispered, "Aye, you pleased me more than I would have imagined. Being here with you not only pleases me but is sheer bliss." She ran her hand across his hard abs. "You, David Drummond, are my Highland bliss."

EPILOGUE

B RADEN GRANT ENTERED THE DRUMMOND great hall with his cousins, Connor and Roddy.

The three found the Ramsay brothers not far from the door. Apparently, they were still discussing the Band of Cousins as they'd done at the wedding. Connor nodded to Braden to indicate he wanted to listen to them for a wee bit, so Braden stood back next to Roddy.

Micheil was busy doing his best to convince Logan and Quade of the group's talents. "Hell, I wouldn't have believed it if I hadn't seen it with my own eyes, Logan."

Logan glanced over the group scattered around the courtyard, speechless, a rare thing for the man known as the beast of the Highlands.

Uncle Quade just laughed. "I kept telling you two this day would come. What a group."

Logan said, "You can thank my two, Maggie and Gavin, for getting this group started. You know they're the best."

"What the hell is wrong with you?" Micheil said. "My two sons led them these past days. Didn't you notice David and Daniel?"

Uncle Quade clapped him on the back. "Micheil, I think you should welcome three members of the group who just arrived, my nephews who did a fine job today. You two will never shut up, will you?"

Micheil's eyes lit up, and he hurried over to them. "Come on in, lads. Glad you could help us celebrate David and Anna's wedding. We've sent them off on their own, but 'tis a night for celebrations, for the cousins, and for all the Drummond clan. You are welcome to spend the night. There's a chamber above stairs with three pallets for you."

Diana greeted them each individually. "Connor, you look so much like your sire, and I swear you must be taller than him by now."

Connor smiled, for he was always pleased to be compared to his sire, Alex Grant, renowned as the greatest swordsman in the Highlands. "I believe we have reached the same height."

Roddy was next. She gave him a quick hug and said, "Roddy, you are the spitting image of your mother, but you have your sire's fair hair. You Grant lads are such a joy to have with us. Thank you for assisting David in this endeavor, whatever you did. He'll be ready to work with the cousins again once he's back home. We've found a nice cottage for the two of them in the farthest corner of the bailey. 'Twill give them a wee bit of privacy before the day comes when he takes over for me and moves back into the keep."

Braden wondered what she would say to him. He was the shortest lad in the Band of Cousins, and while he adored his cousins, he knew he had trouble keeping up with their prowess in the lists.

"And Braden, I hear you did a wonderful job as the negotiator at the waterfalls. I've heard you are a formidable power with that sword of yours, and 'tis said your fists are even more powerful, but your skill in reasoning with a daft man is impressive. How did you know what to say to keep him talking?"

Connor laughed. "Och, he told the lad that he'd take him to the Highlands and give him whatever he wanted."

"Aye, I told him what he wanted to hear. Whatever I could think of to distract him and give David time to climb up the ravine," Braden replied. He couldn't help but have his chest puff out a little. He hadn't expected anyone to congratulate him on what he'd done because it had been a small part of a group effort. "We work well together, 'tis the important part we learned."

Roddy held a goblet up and said, "I'll drink to that."

Diana said, "You drink up, lads. You deserve it, and you have plenty of cousins here to entertain you." Then Diana surprised him even more when she leaned closer to whisper, "Besides, Braden, I hear you drive the lassies daft with your good looks."

He was so stunned, he couldn't think of a word to say. Fortunately, Micheil saved him.

Micheil clasped Braden's shoulder and said, "Eat hearty, lads. Please enjoy yourselves. Your chamber is at the end of the passageway to the right. We gave you David's chamber and threw two pallets on the floor."

Micheil and Diana left to greet more people coming in through the doors. Connor said, "I'm grabbing a meat pie and heading into the courtyard. I saw Gavin and Gregor head that way. Gavin is always good for a laugh."

Braden followed his cousins, surprised at the number of guests gathering inside the hall. It wasn't as big as the Grant great hall, but it was well cared for and clean. The chairs and tables showed exquisite woodworking, and the tapestries on the walls were rich and luxurious. Clan Drummond clearly had great wealth.

The gathering continued outside. A multitude of people from the Drummond village stood about imbibing and eating, laughing and bragging. Braden followed his cousins across the courtyard to a group gathered around a bench. Gavin's voice carried to them, talking about how the cousins had taken Ossian down.

Braden stopped to grab another meat pie at a booth the Drummonds had set up in the courtyard. He leaned down to see if the filling was mutton or rabbit when a shoulder nearly pushed him face first into the meat pies.

His temper flared, but he forced himself to calm down. It certainly wouldn't do to stir up trouble at his cousin's celebration. Nonetheless, he spun around to look at the offender. A man a head taller than Braden glared at him. "Hurry up so I can grab my share."

"I'll take my time, arse."

"Hellfire you won't." He had brown hair and broad shoulders, but his eyes told Braden he loved to taunt others. Bully—a big bully. "Get out of my way."

Braden was smaller than the fool, aye, but he wasn't intimidated.

The man grabbed Braden's tunic by the neck and lifted him off his feet. Braden counteracted with his fist, delivering a blow that landed with a resounding crack, causing the bastard to let go of him, stand back, and grab his nose. The brute only hesitated a moment, but that was all Braden needed to grab the idiot's leg and toss him onto his back. "I said I'll take my time."

The man glared at him but held his hands back. "My apologies. Take what you want and move on." The look in his eyes told him this wasn't over, though perhaps the man was wise enough not to start a fight with a courtyard full of Ramsays, Drummonds, and Grants.

Braden stood back, surprised to see a beautiful woman reach for the man to help him. The boor shoved her hands away.

"Greer, please. Can we not leave?"

Braden felt as though he'd been punched—not by the brute, but by the woman behind him. She was by far the most beautiful lass he'd ever seen. Her golden hair was pulled back at the sides, but the bulk of it tumbled down her back in glorious waves. He couldn't tell the color of her eyes because it was dark and she wouldn't look at him, her gaze instead darting from side to side.

"Don't touch me, Cairstine." He bounced to his feet, never taking his gaze from Braden.

She stepped back and dropped her gaze to the ground. Her dark green wool gown indicated she was of no station, but it also showed the soft curves covered by the coarse fabric.

Hell, but he felt as though he'd been delivered a blow that he would never recover from. He knew it was lust and not love, but hellfire, she'd sent a spark to his loins that he fought to tamp down.

Braden felt someone's arm on his. "Need help, cousin?" Connor asked. Roddy sidled up next to them.

"Nay, I've handled it," Braden replied. He grabbed a meat pie, and the three of them turned away. They hadn't taken two steps from the cart when he heard a resounding slap. He whirled around in time to see the woman with her hand on her cheek.

This time his head nearly exploded. He said, "Did you just hit a lass? Surely a big man like you doesn't need to pick on a wee lass to make himself feel stronger, does he?"

The bully stared at him, a small grin on his face. "Cairstine? Did I hit you?" He had his hand on her wrist.

Cairstine dropped her hand from her face and shook her head. "Nay. He didn't hit me. A bug bit me. I slapped it away."

"Leave it be, Braden," Connor said.

He memorized the bastard's face and his plaid, though he didn't recognize it. He'd find him later. The brute grabbed three meat pies and shoved two at the lass, then yanked her along behind him.

Braden yelled out, "Someone needs to teach you how to treat a lass, arsehole." The man kept going, ignoring his taunt. Turning to Connor, he ground out, "You should have let me at him."

Connor's gaze followed the man out through the gates. "Not here, but I'm betting we'll see him again. I never forget a face."

Daniel popped up next to him, seemingly appearing

from out of nowhere.

"Since you're so talented at traveling about unobserved and picking up information, who is that, Ghost?" Roddy asked Daniel, using the name David had given him. "Were you close enough to get a good look at him?"

Daniel grinned, looking quite proud of himself. "I've seen him before. Lamont. Blair or Greer. They're brothers and they're both nasty."

"Greer. She called him Greer. You must be correct."

Daniel rolled his eyes, and Roddy said, "You doubted him?"

Braden had to laugh. "Nay, Daniel. I'll never doubt you. You certainly do know how to travel unnoticed, Ghost."

Braden and Connor watched the fool toss the woman, his wife no doubt, up onto a horse before he mounted his own.

Braden had a funny feeling come over him, the kind that would often return later, the kind that told him this wasn't the last time he'd see the woman. Destiny, perhaps? "Do you know where their castle is? I think I'll pay him a visit on the morrow," Braden said.

"Nay," Daniel said. "He used to live south of here, but they let their castle fall to ruins, so they left. Don't know where they went."

Roddy grinned. "I think we'll be hunting on the way home. Am I not correct, Braden?"

"Do not worry," Braden whispered. "I'll find him."

Green. Her eyes were green like the newest buds in the spring. She'd glanced at him on the way out. But he'd also noticed something else.

Those green eyes were full of pain, and he vowed to fix that.

THE END

DEAR READERS,

Thank you for reading *Highland Abduction*! This was a different novel for me, but I loved going back to the Drummonds. If you get the chance, check out Drummond Castle. It's known for its beautiful gardens, and though this book is complete fiction, I thought Anna's love for flowers would be a beautiful start for the Drummond Gardens.

If you couldn't tell, Braden's story is next, and I've plotted it out already. I'm hoping you'll love it.

We shall see!

Happy reading, and I so appreciate you following me on this journey.

As always, reviews would be greatly appreciated. Sign up for my newsletter on my website at *www.keiramontclair.com*. I send newsletters out with each new release.

Keira Montclair

www.keiramontclair.com
www.facebook.com/KeiraMontclair/
www.pinterest.com/KeiraMontclair/

RAMSAYS

FAMILY TREE (1280s)

QUADE RAMSAY and wife, BRENNA GRANT
Torrian (Quade's son from his first marriage) and wife, Heather—Nellie (Heather's daughter from a previous relationship) and son, Lachlan
Lily (Quade's daughter from his first marriage) and husband, Kyle—twin daughters, Lise and Liliana
Bethia and husband, Donnan
Gregor
Jennet

LOGAN RAMSAY and wife, GWYNETH
Molly (adopted) and husband, Tormod
Maggie (adopted)
Sorcha and husband, Cailean
Gavin
Brigid

MICHEIL RAMSAY and wife, DIANA
David
Daniel

AVELINA RAMSAY and DREW MENZIE
Elyse
Tad
Tomag
Maitland

Novels by

Keira Montclair

———◆———

THE BAND OF COUSINS
HIGHLAND VENGEANCE

THE CLAN GRANT SERIES
#1- RESCUED BY A HIGHLANDER-
Alex and Maddie
#2- HEALING A HIGHLANDER'S HEART-
Brenna and Quade
#3- LOVE LETTERS FROM LARGS-
Brodie and Celestina
#4-JOURNEY TO THE HIGHLANDS-
Robbie and Caralyn
#5-HIGHLAND SPARKS-
Logan and Gwyneth
#6-MY DESPERATE HIGHLANDER-
Micheil and Diana
#7-THE BRIGHTEST STAR IN
THE HIGHLANDS-
Jennie and Aedan
#8- HIGHLAND HARMONY-
Avelina and Drew

THE HIGHLAND CLAN
LOKI-Book One
TORRIAN-Book Two
LILY-Book Three
JAKE-Book Four
ASHLYN-Book Five
MOLLY-Book Six
JAMIE AND GRACIE- Book Seven
SORCHA-Book Eight
KYLA-Book Nine
BETHIA-Book Ten
LOKI'S CHRISTMAS STORY-Book Eleven

THE SOULMATE CHRONICLES
#1 TRUSTING A HIGHLANDER

THE SUMMERHILL SERIES- CONTEMPO-RARY ROMANCE
#1-ONE SUMMERHILL DAY
#2-A FRESH START FOR TWO
#3-THREE REASONS TO LOVE

REGENCY
THE DUKE AND THE DRESSMAKER

ABOUT THE AUTHOR

KEIRA MONTCLAIR is the pen name of an author who lives in Florida with her husband. She loves to write fast-paced, emotional romance, especially with children as secondary characters in her stories.

She has worked as a registered nurse in pediatrics and recovery room nursing. Teaching is another of her loves, and she has taught both high school mathematics and practical nursing.

Now she loves to spend her time writing, but there isn't enough time to write everything she wants! Her Highlander Clan Grant series, comprising of eight standalone novels, is a reader favorite. Her third series, The Highland Clan, set twenty years after the Clan Grant series, focuses on the Grant/Ramsay descendants. She also has a contemporary series set in The Finger Lakes of Western New York and a paranormal historical series, The Soulmate Chronicles.

Contact her through her website, *www.keiramontclair.com*

Made in United States
North Haven, CT
13 January 2025